———————————— ★ ————————————

The staff and family members were huddled outside the tasting room and all of them saw the EMS workers lift the body out onto the open body bag on a gurney. What was left of Margo's mangled head tore loose from the body and fell to the concrete, leaving just the bloody stump of her neck. Esbeth could see the severed spine, the ends of veins sticking out. Most of the blood had long since poured out into the hopper. The head rolled and came to a rest against the wine press, with one of the EMS men chasing it as it rolled. Both Maggie and Betty Sue fainted at the same moment, nearly colliding as they fell, but neither anywhere near being able to care.

———————————— ★ ————————————

"An intriguing, fast-paced tale that keeps you turning the pages. Hall brings his own unique twist to a cast of colorful Texas characters."

—Ben Rehder, author of *Buck Fever* and *Bone Dry*

"Experience Shakespearean-class family dysfunction with a Texas Hill Country vineyard twist in Russ Hall's newest mystery."

—David Marion Wilkinson, author of *Oblivion's Altar*

NO MURDER BEFORE ITS TIME

RUSS HALL

WORLDWIDE.®

TORONTO • NEW YORK • LONDON
AMSTERDAM • PARIS • SYDNEY • HAMBURG
STOCKHOLM • ATHENS • TOKYO • MILAN
MADRID • WARSAW • BUDAPEST • AUCKLAND

NO MURDER BEFORE ITS TIME

A Worldwide Mystery/May 2005

First published by Five Star.

ISBN 0-373-26529-8

Copyright © 2003 by Russ Hall.
All rights reserved. No part of this book may be reproduced
or transmitted in any form or by any means, electronic or
mechanical, including photocopying, recording or by any
information storage and retrieval system, without permission
in writing from the publisher. For information, contact:
Thorndike Press, 295 Kennedy Memorial Drive,
Waterville, ME 04901 U.S.A.

Printed in U.S.A.

NO MURDER BEFORE ITS TIME

ONE

THE SKY WAS BLACK, swirls of misty clouds sweeping across the spray of stars, then clearing and leaving a silver blade of a sickle moon that looked like it had torn a ripping gash in the night only to have the black fill in again.

Godwin "Win" Castle sat in the truck's driver's seat, where he had been since they arrived. They had watched the over-sized red ball of a sun set through the trees while they waited on the night. His elbow rested out his window, and his trained nose of a winemaster registered the smells of a Texas country night in early June—mesquite, sage, a bit of cedar, but none of the feral smell of the night animals they sought. He let out a deep breath and sighed. He felt a sadness that was laced with a stew of fear and an anger he was not ready to explain, even to himself. The two boys sat impatient but quiet beside him. Kyle, who looked more like his father, was in the middle, next to him. Chaz, stockier and blond, sat with an arm out the passenger window, occasionally spitting out into the night.

Neither boy spoke. The three of them had sat in the truck until the slow ticking of the motor cooling had stopped. Win could hear his own heart beating—thumping inside his chest the way it should, though he felt he could tell it was bruised, battered. Damn thing nearly letting him down, and him only fifty-nine. He was more aware of his own goddamned frailty than he had ever been, and he was not the sort to be pleased by that. It made him want to kick, to yell out at the moon at the top of his voice—just the sort of thing he had been warned he could no longer do.

The boys were not all that young either. Kyle was thirty-seven, Chaz a couple of years younger. But he still thought of them as boys, and they *were* boys, until he said otherwise.

They all sat up straighter on the truck seat when they heard the crunch of gravel and barking of the dogs in the other pickup truck pulling up behind them. The lights were out. Boose was driving the damn thing with no headlights. He had eased all the way back in the lane, probably with a gun on the seat beside him, looking for movement that Win would never be able to see in the pitch of the underbrush. Ordering Boose around at the vineyard by day, the way he had for the past eighteen years, was one thing. Being out with him at night was a whole other thing. The truck slid to a soft stop in the gravel and the dogs began to bark in hysterical excitement, with the same urgency to kill that Win could see behind the pale blue coldness of Boose's eyes at night.

Chaz was reaching for his door handle. Win said, "Give it a minute." The rustling canvas of Chaz's hunting jacket stopped.

The gravel crunched under bootsteps that came up to Win's truck. Boose's closely cropped head leaned down to the window and he looked in at the three of them, measuring them. "You dint have to come out so early," Boose said, his eyes catching some of the icy glitter from the moon. "That old boar won't be stirring this way for a while yet." He had the kind of face that looked like it had been carved out of hard white rock by someone with only part of the right tools.

"Thought we might get an early glimpse," Win said. He turned to the boys. "Might as well get out and have a stretch." The door lights came on and Boose looked away to keep his night eyes as Chaz and Kyle tumbled out one side, Win out his side. Above the sound of their getting out of the truck there was the barking of the dogs, the screech of what Win hoped was an owl, and the snapping flutter of bat wings in the dark, frantically flapping silhouettes against the black sky.

When the truck doors were closed and they all stood around the truck, exposed to the night breezes and their own anxieties, Win said, "Do you have any of your woodsy pithy wisdom for us before the hunt, something like your, 'Don't squat with your spurs on?'"

Boose was still looking over at his own truck where the dogs were throwing themselves against the partially closed windows of the cab. "I never said nothing like that," he said without looking back at them.

"He did tell me once..." Kyle paused, checking to see if Win was going to let him speak "...that good judgment comes from experience, and a lot of that comes from bad judgment."

Boose gave an abrupt snort and walked away from them. He had also told them as much younger boys that you ain't learning anything when your mouth's a-jawing. But neither of them chose to mention that. Boose took hunting as seriously as the loaded guns he carried. He kept walking up along the high deer fence that ran along the vineyard boundary. He carried no light, but was bent low looking for sign, getting very little light from the moon, but not needing much.

Win watched him until he was out of sight. One of the perks of living out in a small county, far enough west of Austin to be clear of any influence from there, was that people treated Win like a squire, as they well might with a twenty-one-thousand-acre spread thick with cattle and a hundred-acre vineyard like a jewel at its center. But none of that seemed to matter much to Boose, who often did as he wanted, only responding to Win's orders when his mood pleased.

As soon as Boose was out of sight, and hearing range, Win turned to his sons. "The two of you think you're up to letting go of the old apron strings yet?"

"What are you saying?" Chaz said.

Kyle moved closer, trying to catch the expression on Win's face. Kyle was the more thoughtful of the two boys, Chaz the aggressive and competitive one. Kyle was a listener, and would take his brother's part. But it was Boose who had gone down to the school grounds back when the boys were in high school and had taken care of Tom Parkins, a bully who had been more than Chaz could handle once he had let his mouth led him into a confrontation. Tom was oversized but was hardly five minutes of work for Boose, though the whole family caught hell from the school when Tom was not fit to play football the rest of the season. Only Win's owning the largest spread in the county had kept Boose out of jail for the thumping he had given Tom.

"It's time we settled a few things among ourselves." Win watched the boys, saw Kyle's shoulders slump while Chaz's face lit up in almost demonic glee in the dim light from the moon.

"Like what?" Chaz was not able to keep the excitement from his voice.

"I'm not going to be around forever. We need to see who's going to be on point carrying on the family name."

"I thought that was settled. Kyle's the oldest. That's how it works, doesn't it?" There was a twist of hope in the question.

"Nothing's settled."

"What?" Kyle had sensed this coming, but showed his shock just the same.

"You heard me."

"I can't believe this." Kyle went to turn away, but fascination and concern made him turn back to his father.

Win started to say something, but stopped when he heard the sound of boots crunching on the gravel coming back to the trucks.

"We need to talk," Kyle said.

Win waved a hand at him, turned toward the sound, and waited until Boose's lean form was visible. Boose was only five foot ten and could not be more than a hundred and forty pounds. But it was all bone and muscle, and he had surprised men over twice his size until anyone local gave him a wide clearance. His eyes were squinting now. It was hard for Win to know how much he had heard; the man had ears like some kind of predator creature.

"You find anything?" Win asked.

Boose gave a jerk with his head back up the fence row. "Sign all over the place back there. That's what's got the dogs all in a lather." He turned his head and shouted over at the truck, "Yo, Spook Daddy, Bitch Dog, Whitey, Chigger. You shut the hell up."

It always bothered Win when Boose called to Chigger, who had been dead three years now. Boose was the last person he would suspect of being sentimental. Win never got a clear answer when he asked about the dog. Boose always said, "He was no bigger than a chigger when he was born, but he had a bigger heart than all these other dogs tied together." But he would not admit to having buried the dog himself on the vineyard property. Win had watched him do it.

The shouting only made the dogs bark louder, and that made Boose smile. Bitch Dog was the toughest of them— was what he called Heinz 114, twice 57. She was junk yard material. Whitey was the black lab, and Spook Daddy was hound, mostly. Boose was proud of the dogs, uncommonly proud. They were all products of local frantic coupling by dogs able to fight to survive, and he had turned them into good working dogs. They reminded him of himself.

"You'd better see to your arms. When I turn those dogs loose we're gonna have a chase on our hands. That boar's been trying to dig his way through at the bottom of the fence and would probably make it through tonight if we don't stop it. I 'spect it's around here close somewheres."

Kyle and Chaz turned toward the truck where their rifles were in the gun rack across the back window.

"Leave the guns there, boys." Win's voice had as much snap as he ever used with them.

"What's going on here?" Boose said.

Win turned to him. "I want you to get those knives I had you put an edge on today."

"You'd better say why first."

"Boose, I don't have to explain things. You know that. Get them."

They stood only two feet apart. Boose looking up into Win's face. But there were sparks in his eyes the moon wasn't putting there.

"Do it," Win said, his tone setting the dogs to barking with even greater hysteria.

Boose stood the way he was for another moment, then finally spun on a foot and sulked over to his truck. "Wouldn't've sharpened 'em if I'd've known..." His words trailed off, lost in the barking.

A cloud passed over the moon and the night got even darker. Boose was back with silent steps, standing still within a foot of Win when the moon appeared again. He held out two thick Army sheaths. Win gave a start when he found Boose as close as he was. But the look of disgust never left Boose's face.

There was not enough light to see if there was any color to Boose's face, but Win supposed there was. He knew by now when he was giving Boose a twist, and how hard.

"Come on, Boose," he said. "You're a sportsman."

"I'm a meat hunter." Boose's words were crisp. "Sports is for folks who ain't ever hungry."

Win took the two Ka-Bar knives and handed one to each of the boys. Chaz snatched his, gripped the serrated leather grip and pulled the knife out of the sheath and looked at the seven-inch blade. Boose had honed them, so Chaz didn't dare run a finger over the edge.

Kyle was reluctant, but finally reached out and took the other knife. "I think we should talk." All his life had been lived under the assumption he would inherit the bulk of the estate, at the very least, half of it. His eyes were searching his father's face in the dim light, looking for signs of madness perhaps. His position was awkward. If he balked, the look he saw said he would miss out entirely. He slowly fastened the sheath to his belt as Chaz had and then went over to the truck to get one of the long-handled flashlights they each carried. When he came back, he said to his father, "When this is over, we still talk."

Win was staring at Boose. "Are you going to turn those dogs loose?"

"I'd better. You may have a lot of influence, but you'll find out just how much out here if you go trying to order other people's dogs around."

Boose turned to Kyle and Chaz, both of whom he had mentored for years in hunting and woods lore. Most of the trophy heads they had mounted back at the house they owed to his training. He said, "If I was you boys I wouldn't do this. You hear me? Getting next to a wild boar even with a gun is nothing to fool with. Going in with just a knife's a damn fool way to get yourselves hurt, hurt bad."

Chaz shrugged, nodded toward his father. Though the night hid the expression on his face, his body language said he was lit up about the notion of a competition between himself and Kyle, and the possible rewards to come from it. Kyle was moving slowly, but had been around his father too long to buck the idea, even if it meant risk. To back down now might mean he'd forfeit everything. There was no telling. He had not seen his father like this in a long time, and could not begin to say what had brought on the mood now.

"Now, Boose, I'm talking to you, not your dogs. Set them loose and let's get these boys on the trail."

"I've heard of hunting boar with just a Ka-Bar before, but if I'd known that was what you were up to, I'd've ground those blades 'til they were good for nothing." But Boose headed over to the truck and opened the cab door. The dogs shot out of the seat; Whitey jumped up at Boose while the other two took off like shots. Then Whitey spun and raced off after them. Boose stood listening to their barks, didn't move again until he heard them pick up the right trail. He would have known if they had veered off the mark and took off after a raccoon.

He reached inside the cab, took a Colt .45 out from under the seat and shoved it into his belt. He slung a Marlin .22 lever-action rifle with a scope over his shoulder and picked up his .243 Weatherby Vanguard bolt-action rifle.

"What's the .22 for?" Win asked.

"Case we see a coon. I saw sign, and a couple of them can eat up eight hundred pound of grapes a season."

"I know that. But don't tell Maggie. She thinks we're catching those in live traps."

"Sometimes we do. Then we kill them." Boose came as close again to a smile as he had all night. "I'll let you do any lying needs to be done to Miss Maggie."

Win turned to Kyle and Chaz. "You boys get started after those dogs. Boose and I'll catch up after a bit. That okay with you, Boose?"

"It ain't none of my funeral."

Chaz made an eager spin in the direction of the barking dogs. He walked into the dark of the night until the beam of his flashlight clicked on, then the ball of light on the ground was the only thing that showed of him.

Boose had his eye on Kyle. He knew Chaz was tom fool enough to go for something like this. But he waited to see if all the years of doing what his father said, of standing in the shadow waiting, and of doing second-rate work had taken all the sand out of Kyle.

Kyle shrugged and turned to head off after Chaz.

Boose let out a long slow puff of air.

"Why don't you just go ahead and tell me what you think, Boose." Win stood with his hands on his hips, watching the two beams of light fade into the underbrush.

"I think all this sucks large lumps of loose gravy," Boose said.

KYLE HURRIED TO catch up with the bobbing flashlight beam that marked Chaz's progress through the underbrush that was getting thicker the farther they went from the fence line. The barking of the dogs came from far to their left ahead.

He called out, "Hold up a minute." But Chaz did not slow down.

The scrub oaks, agarita, and low mesquite plants opened up in a small clearing. Kyle turned off his light and ran until he shot around Chaz. He turned around and flipped his light on, held it so it was to Chaz's face.

"What?" Chaz held a hand up to block the light, and slowed to a stop while he fought to get his vision back.

"Let's not do this. It's nuts."

"You'd say that. Then we're right back where we were."

"Where we always were. But that's not the point. He's not right. Something's up. We should…"

Chaz moved to jerk away from where Kyle held the sleeve of his hunting jacket. Kyle gripped his brother tighter. Chaz's face was turned from him, but Kyle was seeing the face of his wife, Cassie, when he got home and would have to explain to her. Cassie—whom he no longer called Cassandra—was like his mother, Margo, a fierce social climber. If she found out she was at the end of the beanstalk and there was suddenly no treasure, she was going to be a problem. He was not sure what she would do, but he had ideas. Cassie had been a stunning young girl, and was now a beautiful woman. But Kyle had no pretensions about her. She had high standards, and his being principal heir to the Castle estate had weighed in her accepting him. They had no children. Chaz had three kids by his wife, Bea. Win had thrown that in Kyle's face often enough.

"Let's stand up to him. That's what he really wants. Don't you see?"

Chaz jerked his arm free and spun to face Kyle. He was breathing hard, but he said nothing.

"Come on. We're family. And what would Bea say?"

Kyle reached out an arm, heard the slide of steel on steel as Chaz pulled the Ka-Bar knife from its sheath at his belt. He held the knife in one hand and the flashlight in the other. He took a step back. That was Chaz—always ready to act like his back was to the wall. Kyle stepped back, but was not surprised. What was racing through Kyle's deliberative mind was how much his father had been counting on that.

Kyle's eyes fixed on the exposed blade. It was as sharp as any knife Boose had anything to do with, which meant it would go without effort through a tough boar's hide. Chaz spun and started to run in the direction of the dogs' heightened barking. Kyle stood for a stunned moment or two more before he forced himself into motion and pushed himself into a run up the path where stickers grabbed at his jacket and ripped at the backs of his hands.

Boose HAD STOOD POISED to head off after the dogs and the two boys. But Win waved for him to wait a bit longer. So Boose leaned back against the fender of the truck. He looked off into the night, listening to the barking of the dogs on the trail.

The wind picked up in the tops of the trees, the same breeze from the lake that cooled the grapes each evening. Boose seemed to be sniffing at something on the wind. Win tried to smell what Boose was getting, could only get a whiff of lake, the live oaks, and a hint of cedar.

"Are they after a raccoon?"

"No. It's the pig."

"How do you know?"

"I just do."

Boose was always leaning against something or sitting when he wasn't working, though he worked long days at the vineyard, dawn until late evening when critters were stirring after the grapes. Something was often going wrong at the winery too and he was a native problem solver. He possessed the knack for taking things apart and fixing them, and since Win was not fond of buying new machines and appliances, Boose talents were in constant demand for the high maintenance, older gadgets used daily. But Boose's skills were limited to fixing the machines. He was less apt with people. A flurry of five wives who had come and gone in his life had helped drive that message home to him. Though he had some raw animal magnetism for women, he had quit encouraging them and stayed with his hunting and work at the vineyard.

After a few minutes, Boose turned his head toward Win and looked at him with a careful scan. "Everything all right with you?" he asked.

Win frowned. Though Boose had been with him for years, Win did not encourage personal conversations. He did not mind belaboring the details of the work day, but had little else to share. He surprised Boose this time by saying, "Why do you ask?"

"'Cause you're acting damn-all strange is why. Ever since you disappeared for a week, back a month ago, you come back all wound up like some over-worked watch.

Now this clap-trap stuff." Boose nodded toward where the boys had headed off and gave a low snort.

Win stared back at the glare he was getting from Boose. He damn well was not going to tell Boose what bothered him. Only Margo knew, not even Kyle and Chaz. Win let his eyes drift away from Boose out to the night.

Boose stood up and away from the fender and looked over into the night woods. The barking of the dogs had changed. "We'd better go now," he said.

"Give it a bit more." Win stood looking up at the stars, as if there was some kind of answer up there. When he looked back he could see that Boose's glare had become even more hostile. Win asked, "What would you do if you were one of my sons?"

Boose never blinked. He looked at Win and said, "I'd find me a load-bearing wall, and I'd press you up against it. Then I'd knock your teeth so far down your throat your asshole'd be wearing a picket fence."

"I ought to fire you for talking to me like that."

"Yeah, but you won't or you'd've had the balls to do it years ago."

"By God, I wish either of my boys had your spine, I really do."

"You shoulda let me have a go at the Missus a long time ago if that was what you had in mind."

"By God, Boose…"

"I know. I know. You oughta fire me. Well, do it for going after my own damn dogs." He spun and started off into the night, the dogs' leashes and a stretch of rope over his shoulder beside the .22. A long flashlight was tucked into his belt, but he did not turn it on or use its light. Yet he seemed to know where he was going, following the tracks Win's sons had made.

Win waited until the crunch of Boose's boots had faded into the dark. He opened the door of his truck, reached under the seat, and pulled out a bottle of Cabernet Sauvignon with a cork sticking out of its neck. He pulled the cork and swished the bottle. The bottle was half empty. He hated not to drink from a glass, but hell, he felt far from civilization at the moment. He lifted the bottle and drank until it was empty. Then he put the cork in and threw the bottle off into the thickest of the brush. He took a tin of ALTOIDS from his pocket, popped a couple of "curiously strong" mints into his mouth, then turned on his flashlight and hurried after Boose.

THE BARKING OF THE DOGS hit a new hysterical high, then the barking stopped. All Kyle could hear were growls and an occasional yip. Chaz had burst ahead. His light flickered through the mesquite trunks and broke into sparkles of yellow light through the dense brush. Kyle hurried to catch up and stumbled into a chest-high clump of prickly pear cactus that spread for fifty feet across his path. He eased around to the left of it, found his way blocked by a tight knot of impenetrable vines binding stickery locust limbs into a wall. Kyle beat his arm against the mess and only made things worse by scratching himself and getting entangled for a minute. He wrenched himself free and turned and ran, but was forced to go all the way to the right of the cacti and now could barely see Chaz's light far up ahead. He could hear the dogs growling, though, and the occasional snort and squeal of the boar.

Kyle drew his knife and thrashed with it and his flashlight, beating a way through the brush as he ran, stumbling toward the noise. He was pushing through another thick wall of stickery limbs when the shrubs gripping him let go and he stumbled out into a clearing. Chaz was darting around the thrashing black shape that was the boar, trying to get an opening to dive in closer. They were less than twenty yards away. Kyle rushed toward them. As he got closer he saw that Bitch Dog and Spook Daddy each had a grip on one of the pig's ears. Whitey had locked his big teeth on a hind leg and clung to it as the boar whirled, trying to cut at the dogs with its long white curved tusks.

Chaz looked up and saw Kyle getting closer. He jumped suddenly onto the back of the boar, which was far from being tired. The sudden extra weight on his back threw the boar into a heightened frenzy, its head whipping from left to right; the dogs were lifted off the ground and tossed each way. Chaz's arm rose and fell. Kyle ran forward. It was hard to tell if the blade was penetrating the boar's tough hide. When he was right up at the fray Kyle saw the blade going in, but could not tell if Chaz was getting to the boar's heart. The thick black line of bristles that ran up the pig's spine was a blur as the boar spun, its slashing head reaching back for Chaz's legs. Chaz bent forward, a fistful of the thick bristles in his fist. He slashed the sharp blade along the boar's neck, and a spray of blood shot up from the fight across the dogs and the trunk of a live oak.

Chaz may have let up, thinking the animal would drop

now. As soon as he relaxed, the animal jerked to the side, banging Spook Daddy against the tree. The white tusks dipped and slashed up Chaz's pant leg, lifting him two feet into the air.

Kyle dropped his flashlight and knife, rushed forward and grabbed the boar's other hind leg. He lifted and jerked, pulling the pig away from his brother. Chaz fell over, rolling on the ground to get away. The pig's head lowered, but Kyle jerked again and the boar thumped onto its side, struggling at once to get back to its feet.

A blur of motion came in from Kyle's left. With his and Chaz's lights on the ground it was hard to make out Boose. But he heard him yell, "Give him hell, Chigger."

There Boose was, a dim shadow, stepping forward with the .45 extended in one hand.

"Boom." The blast ripped the night apart. "Boom. Boom." The pig rolled onto its side and stopped kicking. The dogs didn't let up, but Boose was busy yanking them off and clicking their leashes into place. When he had all three, he jerked and yelled at them, calling out their names. Whitey would not let go until Boose gave him a sound kick along the side of his ribs. Then he was able to pull the dogs away and run the long loop of rope he carried around the trunk of the oak.

Chaz lay on the ground. Kyle went over to him, saw the blood along the tear in his jeans. He bent closer, held out a hand. Chaz waved it away for the moment and lay there. Kyle looked up and saw his father coming into the clearing with his flashlight sweeping from the boar, to the dogs, then to his two sons.

"I wish you hadn't shot it," Chaz said to Boose. "I wanted the head as a trophy."

Win looked over at Kyle. There was the sadness from earlier, and a bit of firmness now.

Boose was bent over Chaz and was cutting away one leg of his jeans, exposing a long gash that ran from the side to the back of Chaz's thigh. He tore the jeans material into strips and started tying them over the wound.

Boose stood up as soon as he had the bleeding stopped for the moment. "We'd better get him back to the house," he said.

Win was standing by the boar, shining his light down on it. Blood was shiny wet in smears on the thick black fur. The white curled upper and lower tusks on this side stuck up like bent knives of bone.

Boose looked away, over to where the dogs had settled down a bit once they found they could no longer get to the pig. Bitch Dog was licking at her rump where she had a small gash from one of the slashing tusks. Whitey looked alert, but more eager to play now than hunt. Spook Daddy had curled up, his head across one paw, staring at the dead boar. "You're a sorry lot of dogs, you are," Boose said to them. "That damned Chigger'd still be hanging onto a hind leg right now. I'd be having to get the 'jaws-of-life' to wrench him loose."

Win went over to help Chaz to his feet. Kyle took the other side.

"Give us a hand here, Boose," Win said. "No one wants to hear about your damn ghost dog just this second."

TWO

THE TRUCK SLID to a stop in the gravel. Win threw open his door and rushed around to help Kyle with Chaz. Margo stood in the doorway to the house, watching them help Chaz from Win's pickup truck. The light that washed the red tiles of the courtyard white did not reveal her expression. "Take him to the tasting room," she shouted. "I'll call and then bring the first aid kit." She turned back into the house and closed the door on them.

The house, winery, and separate tasting room were patterned in miniature after the Château Mouton-Rothschild in the Bordeaux region of France. Margo had taken certain liberties with the courtyard, using Spanish tiles, and she had tucked the tasting room's parking area off to the side so that visitors got a good look at this end of the huge Lake Fredonia, which was responsible for the constant breezes that swept the vineyard each day and evening. All the old world charm and high ceilings went with the place, but with the latest technology, lighting, and conveniences. They were a good fifty miles from the nearest large city, though, and with that went the services of the best hospitals.

Chaz had an arm over Win's and Kyle's shoulders. The trio turned and started for the building across the courtyard from the house, with Chaz hopping on one leg as they went. Win dug in a pocket to get the key ready. Chaz was breathing slowly, his athletic conditioning showing, though he had lost quite a bit of blood and was starting to shiver.

Win unlocked the tasting room and turned on the lights, then went back to the doorway to help Chaz inside. They lowered him to the floor just as Boose's truck pulled into the lot, the dogs still barking in excitement over the recent taste of blood.

Blood had seeped through the torn jean wrappings on Chaz's leg that Boose had fashioned in the woods. Win knew that was why Margo had ordered them in here. These tile floors would be easier to clean of blood than anything inside the house. Win glanced around, spotted a couple of tablecloths.

"You get some water, Kyle," Win said. He began tearing one of the tablecloths into strips. "We need to clean the wound."

Kyle brought over a small dish of water and Win began to dab at the wound. "Get some blankets from the house," he told Kyle. "Ones your mother won't care about."

Margo came inside the tasting room as Kyle shot out.

"That's a stupid waste," she snapped when she saw what he'd done with the tablecloth. She squatted down with the first aid kit and nudged Win out of the way. He rose and went over to the chest-high marble bar that ran along one wall. He reached over and got one of the bottles that had been opened for tastings. It was Merlot. He pulled off the rubber seal where air had been pumped out of the bottle, reached for one of the glasses, and poured himself a full glass.

"Do you want a glass, Chaz?"

Before he could answer, Margo said, "Don't be a fool. I called for StarFlight. They won't want him full of liquor when they get him in the E.R."

"We could have taken him in once we got him patched up."

Margo frowned at Win. "It's a fifty-mile trip. They didn't want to come at first, but I told them who was calling. Your name's still good for one or two things around here."

Kyle opened the door and came in with an armload of blankets. Maggie and Boose followed him inside the tasting room. Boose hung back by the door. Maggie rushed forward, her face flushed. "Oh, my God. Chaz. What happened?"

"Stay back, dear, and give him a chance to breathe." Margo waved a hand at Maggie without looking at her. She went back to patching up the tear in his leg.

"What caused it?"

"Your father being an idiot."

"That's not…"

"Shut up, Win."

Kyle stood up from putting the blankets on the floor beside Chaz, and Maggie got her first look at Chaz's leg. The leg seemed unusually pale, except where a trickle of blood ran down from a butterfly suture Band-Aid her mother had just put in place. Maggie reeled back a step, held out a hand to steady herself on one of the counters displaying wine racks, stemmed glasses, and other wine-related merchandise.

"Oh, my God," she said. Maggie was only twenty-three, a dozen years younger than Chaz—an afterthought Margo had called her, although Win had said a mistake. "He's hurt, hurt bad. What is it?"

"His hamstring," Boose said. "Kinda ironic, ain't it."

Margo stopped what she was doing and looked up at Boose. "Isn't there something you should be doing?"

"Yeah, but outta politeness I'm not gonna do it." But he spun on his boot heel and went back outside.

"That man is getting far too insolent." Margo went back to patching Chaz's leg.

"We can't fire him," Win said.

"Yeah, he's like family," Maggie said, "one of us."

"Don't go too far, dear," her mother said.

"We'd have our hands full if he ever did leave and decided to get chatty," Kyle said. He was public relations manager for the vineyard in addition to having the eastern half of Texas as his sales territory. "We haven't done anything criminal, but we've cut some corners with the wine we wouldn't want the buying public to know about."

Win refilled his glass, glanced over at Kyle, but did not say anything.

Margo finished putting the butterfly sutures on the leg wound and leaned back on her haunches for a moment.

Maggie pressed closer. "Why did you say Dad was being an idiot?"

"We don't need to go into that," Win said.

Margo glared at Win, then turned back to Maggie and the two boys. "You kids might as well know…."

"Margo." Win's voice boomed, but she ignored it.

"Your father had a heart attack last month. That's where we were, not on the sudden vacation like all of you thought."

"I told you not to…."

"It's making him act screwy. I don't know what to think about his behavior. He's been a mess ever since. We owe him sympathy, but we don't have to be fools too."

"Don't talk about him like that." Maggie's voice had gone up an octave.

Kyle was looking at his father differently. Chaz lay with his head against the cool tiles.

Maggie stared at Win, her lower lip began to quiver. "Oh, Dad." She looked like she wanted to reach out to him.

Win spun and went out the door. Boose was standing outside in the dark looking off at the horizon. Win stopped to stand in the night breeze and quiet beside him.

"What is it?" Win said. Then he heard the distant "whop, whop, whop" sound of the helicopter. It had only been twenty-five or thirty minutes since Margo had called, but the Castle name must have lit a fire with someone who mattered.

"Guerney Simmons chopped his whole leg off and they wouldn't send no helicopter after him," Boose said.

"That was back before they had StarFlight," Win corrected. "They would probably have come for that."

"Won't make no difference to Guerney. Bled to death."

The two men were silent for a while, Win taking an occasional sip from his glass as the sound of the helicopter increased. A gust of wind lifted the front lock of Win's gray hair and tossed it.

Boose gave him a sideways glance. "Everything going all right with you?"

"A little setback is all," Win said.

Anything either might have said after that was drowned out by the roar of the whirring blades as the helicopter swept over the grounds and shined a light across to find an open field for a landing.

"THAT BREEZE YOU FELT coming off Lake Fredonia is the main reason the Castles decided to begin a vineyard after their tour of the finest grape-growing vineyards of France. That and the sandy, loamy earth that gives the vines a high mineral soil and such good drainage." Esbeth Walters led the tour group of two young couples and four retired ladies into the tasting room. The cool of the air conditioning inside washed over her like a wave of ocean water after the 97-degree blast of sun outside. The room was a high-ceiling open-space area with displays of merchandise on tables and shelves along the walls and with a marble-top bar and sales counter that ran the length of one wall. The room smelled of wine, like a gentle cloud of Chardonnay hovering in the room. The retired ladies beat the young couples up to the tasting bar. One of them, who wore a pink baseball cap, was already asking for something red and sweet, a request Esbeth was going to have to disappoint, since all of the Camelot Hills red wines were dry.

Esbeth was a retired lady herself, a seventy-two-year-old one who felt much younger when not in a crabby mood. She had been a school teacher and she still ran into grown students now and again who had studied math under her direction. A few months back she had grabbed at the chance to give tours through the winery, even though it meant a very long drive to the vineyard every other day. But the opportunity to meet people and chatter a bit was doing her worlds of good. It pleased her as much to have that nosy biddy Mrs. McCorkle next door find excuses to be out on her lawn and to see Esbeth pull out of the drive each time without knowing where Esbeth was headed. She bet that scalded the old goat's preserves. Mrs. McCorkle was barely sixty herself, thought she knew everything, and was far too willing to share her pearly wisdom.

Esbeth stepped around a recent stain on the tiles that did not look like it was made by wine. The doings on the grounds last night had been the talk of the winery. Esbeth was still having a hard time picturing Win and Margo as impetuous young lovers, seeing the sun set over rows of vines in France so long ago, holding hands and looking into each other's eyes, then rushing back to their inn to have a fumbling go at perhaps conceiving one of the two boys that were the blessing and curse of the estate right now, if she understood the rumors.

"Now we get to the best part," Esbeth steered the group over to the tasting bar, saw that Pearl was ringing up a sale at the far end of the marble-top counter. "We get to taste the wines." She reached into the cooler and pulled out the first chilled bottle of wine, a Sauvignon Blanc. "We start with the drier white wines first, to give your taste buds a chance. We'll work our way through three other wines with a bit more residual sugar, then we'll get to a couple of the reds."

The couples sniffed at their glasses and then sipped at the wine, while the lady in the pink ball cap knocked hers back like it was a shot of rye whiskey. "Tastes like the back of a postage stamp," she said.

Esbeth yanked her eyes away from the woman. Betty Sue, the office manager, came in and went over to talk in low tones with Pearl. Esbeth said, "Sauvignon Blanc is meant to be dry and have an abrupt finish. That way it lets an entrée like Dover Sole show off its sauce."

"What goes good with hot dogs and sauerkraut?" It was the lady in the hat again. The women with her giggled. But the hat lady said, "It's what we're having tonight. I just wanna know."

Esbeth was trying hard to hear what Betty Sue was saying to Pearl. Whatever it was, Pearl looked ready to cry. Then Betty Sue gave Pearl a pat on the shoulder and went back outside and across the courtyard to the house where there was an office for the winery.

"Well?" the woman asked again.

Esbeth looked back, forced her eyes away from the bright cap, and said, "We make a spicy mustard with our Chenin Blanc wine. You might try that on the hot dogs along with the kraut, and then have a chilled bottle of the Chenin Blanc."

That shut the heckler up for a bit, especially when Esbeth got to the Chenin Blanc and the woman discovered its residual sugar level made it the sweetest wine they would try.

Esbeth worked her way through the rest of the tasting and sent the folks down the counter to buy their wine selections from Pearl. But her mind was on whatever was bugging Pearl, as well as on the strange Castle family. The whole bunch of Castles had a tinge of arrogance that always put her off a bit. It was subtle, like a brick in a velvet glove. Only Margo made the superficial attempt to be gracious, but her phony laugh and gratuitous chatter was not the balm she might have thought it was. Esbeth felt a whole lot more comfortable around folks like Boose and his sister Pearl.

When the current group left the tasting room, it was quiet except for the clink of glass as Esbeth put the Camelot Hills bottles back into the cooler. She left the reds out at room temperature, but slipped the rubber stoppers into place since they had all had time to breathe and dissipate the taste of tannin.

The past few times she had been out to the winery to give tours, Esbeth had felt the heightened tension. But she figured that was normal for small businesses with lots of family members involved. All the Castles worked at the winery, as well as Boose and his sister, Pearl.

She watched Pearl counting the cases of wine again, a clipboard in one hand. Her face pink, she was working with uncharacteristic antic energy, banging around, opening and closing cabinets.

"What's the matter, Pearl?"

Pearl straightened up from where she was bent over under the counter. "We're missing another case of wine."

"Red again?"

"Yeah. Betty Sue says Margo insists it'll come out of my salary if I can't account for it. They did put me in charge of the tasting room, but I can't imagine…"

Pearl had a perfect round country face, normally with perfect skin glowing with the sheen of a pearl, though it now had a tinge of pink. Esbeth wished Pearl's folks were still around to see how prophetic their name for her had become.

"Take a deep breath, Pearl. It may have nothing to do with us. We're not the only ones with keys to this room. Two of the doors were unlocked when I opened up today."

"After what went on last night, it's no wonder." Pearl shook her head, looked down at the clipboard where the numbers had not changed. "I can't afford this, even at our discount, and I don't even drink."

"I know." Esbeth also knew that Pearl had a three-year-old son and an ex-husband against whom there was a restraining order. "We'll think of something." She had already decided she would talk to Betty Sue, have the amount taken from her own pay slip.

"But you don't need the money like me," Pearl sighed.

"You're right." Esbeth patted her hips. "I just come out for the exercise before someone sends me off to the home for the criminally fat."

"You're not fat."

"No. Just cushioned well against a fall, eh." Esbeth didn't mind being the brut of whatever took Pearl's mind off the missing case, though Pearl's face was still twisted with concern.

Esbeth knew of no rule that said people have to get

harder as they get older. She had seen plenty of people go the other direction, get softer, sentimental, emotional. But Win and Margo Castle must have stood in the Texas sun and baked for all their years. They were sure crispy.

Now Pearl, she leaned the other way. She was too young to know it, but she did. She might have her moments of seeming firm and businesslike on the exterior, but there was that side of her that had led her to be victimized by the likes of Rory Abrams, a standing mass of twitching toe jam if Esbeth had ever met one. Pearl's nature was to her credit. It was what allowed her to weather life and nurture her three-year-old Collin through the small storms of country living.

When Pearl started to look down at her clipboard again, Esbeth asked, "Have you heard anything about Chaz?"

"Just that he's okay, stitched up, and already back at his house. It wasn't that big of a deal, just one of those stupid guy things."

Esbeth took a deep breath herself and looked away but did not respond to that. She changed the subject once again. "How come Boose is named the way he is, for a caboose, when you were the last of the thirteen kids your folks had?"

"I guess I was an afterthought, the way Miss Maggie was." Pearl grinned.

While she was still saying it, Esbeth looked out the nearest window and saw the young Castle daughter, Maggie, coming across the courtyard toward the tasting room. Esbeth hoped the frown the girl wore was from the heat, because she was due to be married next week and it was no time for heavy frowning.

As soon as Maggie was inside the room she could see that Pearl and Esbeth were between crowds. She waved at Pearl and said, "Esbeth, can I see you for a minute?"

Now Esbeth frowned, caught herself, and stopped. She went outside with Maggie, let the young girl lead the way over to a bench in the shade beneath two blooming crepe myrtle plants.

"I'm worried, Esbeth." Maggie was attractive in a classic way that showed she was her mother's daughter. But having been born as a Castle, she had never developed the social climbing frenzy that still gave her mother's face a hard edge when relaxed.

"What about?" But Esbeth was thinking, why tell me? She had only known Maggie a few weeks. Surely the girl had better confidants. "Not your wedding, I hope?"

"No."

"That's all that should be on your mind right now."

"Well, it's Father. I knew he's been acting a bit strange. Now I find out he's had a heart attack and didn't even tell any of us kids. If Mom hadn't been mad at him, we still wouldn't know."

"I still don't understand what's worrying you."

"Everyone knows that just a year or so ago you helped a sheriff find out who killed that fellow that was all chopped up."

"It was Jake Marston, and I found his arm in my coreopsis bed, the only reason I got involved. I wasn't trying to be meddlesome."

"But you'd solved another mystery before that, hadn't you?"

"If you mean the Ferguson case, the police were just as appreciative of my help as the sheriff was." She didn't try to hide her sarcasm.

"But you did solve it."

"So everyone says. What are you beating around about?"

"I just wonder if you could keep an eye on Dad. I mean, I could pay you if you do detective work and charge a fee or anything."

"Honey, I appreciate the unflinching confidence, but I never got paid, nor was I even asked to help out on anything where I did butt in. I'm just a nosy old sort when it comes to something shoved under my nose that doesn't make sense. Some people would call me an amateur detective. The law I dealt with had a handful of less flattering phrases for it. Besides, I usually have to have a murder to sink my teeth into."

Maggie shook her head. "Well, I hope it doesn't come to that. Of course, if I was ever going to murder someone around a winery, I'd use poison." She paused, and got herself back on track. "Does my father's behavior lately make sense to you?"

"I don't know that I can say." Esbeth for some reason was thinking about King Lear.

"I mean, he's pitting Kyle and Chaz against each other. Do you have any idea what that might be about?"

"No. But I'll be the first to admit that men in general have a lot of unopened pages to me. I was never married. Maybe in a few years you can tell me a thing or two."

"What makes men act the way they do?"

"You've got me there. It's the question of the ages. But my guess is that any answer involving puppy dog tails is overplayed."

Maggie's face wrinkled and she looked ready to cry. "Oh, I wish we could just be back the way we were."

Esbeth tried to comfort her. "Maybe everything will smooth out when all of you fly down to Belize for that wedding of yours. I'll bet that will be just one beautiful event."

"Let's hope," Maggie said. But she was looking away, and did not sound confident.

WIN CASTLE SAT brooding at the desk in the small cupola on top of the chateaux residence. He frowned and bent to pull open the cardboard flaps of the case of wine at his feet. He took out a bottle, tore off the foil, and began removing the cork. From here he could look out and see across the rows of vineyard aligned to get the maximum effect from the evening breeze. Five years ago, after an unseasonal winter freeze took out two-thirds of the vines, Bill Markley, his general manager and assistant winemaster, had suggested putting the vines up on a lyre system. It made more work for Boose's crew of Hispanic workers, since they had to tie and train the vines onto wires up into a canopy, but it left the clusters of grapes hanging below the vines in a way that maximized the effect of the breeze, made hand-picking the grapes easier, and made it harder for leaf hoppers and other insects to get onto the vines. The effect from high above the house in the cupola was combed rows of green turning amber in the bath of light from the sun that was dropping over the horizon.

Win could see out across the width of Lake Fredonia from here. The view used to please him, but nothing seemed to please him now. He had been a damned fool to let Bill talk him into the new lyre system for the vines. He wanted them to look the way they had, the way he had seen vines back when he was first looking at vineyards in France. He wanted a lot of things to be the way they had been. That was the whole damned problem.

He heard light footsteps coming up the spiral metal stairs that led from the first floor fermentation room up through the second floor office and den to the smaller cupola office where he came when he wanted to be alone. He grabbed for the open bottle of wine, slipped it back into the case, and shoved the opened case under the desk with one foot.

"I thought I'd find you up here." Margo's head came into sight. Her eyes darted at once over to the wine bottle on the antique sidecar against the wall. She marked the bottle each day with a pen and could see from where she stood that only one glass of wine had been poured.

"What do you want?" Win's voice had a surly edge to it.

"To find out what's wrong with you." She had been very beautiful once, still had the poise of the successful social climber she had been. But she no longer held any attraction for Win. She was just there.

"You know," Win said.

"All I know is about you being a brick-headed fool, but why take it out on the boys?"

"It's more important now that the strong genes run the place."

"I could run it if you're gone."

Win let out a snort of air, but otherwise did not dignify her comment with a response.

"If you want Chaz to run things, why don't you just say so? Chaz has your ruthlessness. He's always been your favorite. Don't make a game out of it."

"This is no game."

"No. I'm afraid it isn't."

He stared out past her at the dimming sky.

"And didn't the doctor tell you no drinking?"

"He said moderate." He turned to her slowly and glared.

Margo sighed. "I just hope you won't spoil the wedding. We spent too much time preparing for it to have you and the testosterone cowboys screw things up."

He didn't answer. After a minute she turned and started back down the stairs.

Win had just enough time to refill his glass when he heard footsteps coming up the stairwell again. What the hell was the good of having a retreat if every damn fool in the house didn't know to leave him alone?

This time it was Kyle.

"Dad, we need to talk."

"No we don't." Win took another drink from his wine glass, felt the alcohol stirring through him, just about the only good thing he had going for him. He would be damned if he would let some hired hand of a doctor try to take that away.

"Cassie's giving me…"

"But what do *you* think?" Win cut him off. "I like that girl, she has something I hoped would have rubbed off. You know, she's kind of a cheerleader with spurs. She's what we need, even if she hasn't given issue. Are you sure you're..."

Kyle stopped his dad from where he was going with that. The cattleman side of Win could get as frank as someone breeding livestock if Kyle let him. Kyle's eyes looked pained. He said, "I thought we had an understanding. And if you're dead set on some sort of competition, why not look at our sales? My numbers are way over Chaz's, always have been. You can ask Clive."

"Clive Abramson is paid to supervise you two, not spend time proving anything to me. And you know that the east side of Texas includes Austin, San Antonio, and Houston. Of course your numbers are better than Chaz's."

"I mean increases, percentages. Look at those. Besides, Chaz has Dallas-Fort Worth and a lot of other big cities in his half of the state. I'm still beating him at that."

"I'm not open to argument about it," Win said. There was a whine to Kyle's voice that put the fingernails to the chalkboard for him. Couldn't the boy see that?

"But you're not going to let last night..."

"You'll have your chance. It's not over yet."

"What do you mean?"

"You'll see when we get to the islands. Just pack your fishing gear, both of you."

"I hope you're not going to let some fish decide my fate," Kyle said.

"We'll see," his father said, and looked away. "We'll see."

THREE

"Mom LOOKED just about as pissed as I've ever seen her."
Kyle was standing beside the console and was knocked
back to the seat behind it by the momentum when Win
pushed the throttle up in a sudden jerk. Water shot up
along the sides of the thirty-two-foot rental boat in a wall
of spray on either side as Win hit the throttle the moment
they cleared the NO WAKE zone. Kyle looked back and
watched the breakwater and slim masts of the moored
yachts fade into the pale sky as the boat surged away from
the shoreline. The taller buildings stood out pink and bright
white against the tropical sun, but they began to grow
smaller as the boat climbed the swells heading out to
deeper water. Soon the coconut trees were reduced to a thin
line of darker green between the pale blue sky and the lime
green water.

"You mean drunk?" Win shouted back at him. None of
the beauty of the tropical setting seemed to have any affect on him.

"No. Upset. You know what I mean." Kyle found himself shouting back and stopped himself. Maggie had been
caught up in the reception, hadn't seen Win grab the boys
and scoot for the door the way Margo had. But Maggie
would be just as upset when she found Kyle and Chaz had

skipped on their wives and were in a fishing boat while the guests were still slamming back wedding champagne.

Kyle glanced over at Chaz who, like himself, wore shorts, a T-shirt, and deck shoes. A thick white wrap was around Chaz's thigh. Other than a slight limp he did not seem too bothered by the wound that was now a bit over a week old. Chaz grinned back at him, the spray pulling his blond hair back, making it a dark mat. The grin was his "I'm going to stand on your throat if I can" kind of grin that Kyle knew so well from their sibling rivalry as small boys, only it looked more dangerous now.

The sky went dark, then light, then dark again as clouds began to mass and drift across the path of the sun. It had rained on and off for the past three days, but had not really kicked up and stormed yet. Today the chances of some kind of serious storm looked better. The sea chopped up into five- and six-foot waves, sending the boat up and down green hills of water. Kyle looked back toward the land and could no longer see the city, though he could make out the Maya Mountains rising in dark mounds to the far west.

Win was following the course he had set during their scouting trips before the wedding. Kyle knew exactly where they were headed, out around the barrier reef for a run down to a tangle of islands where the big sharks would be nosing around in the flats. They had spotted plenty on the most recent outing—a fishing expedition that had lit the fuse that would now have his mother exploding.

Once they were away from the shore and through a buoy-marked cut in the reef and out of sight of the city, Kyle saw only one other boat, an oil tanker far in the distance that came into view each time they rose to the peak of a swell. There were usually more scuba divers and other tourists out among at the thousand or so cays and small islands. The weather had to be a factor. Easterly winds whip up all through June and cause steady showers, usually short and warm ones. But an occasional thunderhead cloud left over from May will loom, and one or two seemed to be in the sky today and headed their way.

The boat bounced across the crests of waves, dipped down into the next one only to lift again. Kyle saw two dolphins leap in the distance, and caught a glimpse of either a manta ray or a big loggerhead turtle beneath the waves as they raced on.

The days of scouting before the wedding had turned all their faces a dark red. Looking at his father, steady at the wheel and staring ahead at each wave set, it was hard to believe he could not go toe to toe with anything, that his heart was really frail and ready to collapse. But it had let him down once. He seemed to be using all that was left of himself, driving himself with an Ahab-like frenzy that Kyle could not begin to understand. Win should be relaxing back under one of those coconut palms by the pool instead of being out here pressing himself and the boys on some quest for sharks just to settle whatever gnawing personal doubt seemed to have sprouted in the past few weeks. It was hard to think of his father as a bit crazy. But, looking at the firm clamp of his father's jaw and his white-knuckled grip on the boat's wheel, Kyle would have hated to be asked to vote on that just this second.

Win ran the boat down along the outside of a long barrier reef until it broke up and small islands were scattered in low dots across the top of the water. They were within a mile or two of where they had done their best barracuda fishing the day before when the storm hit.

Big drops of water smacked against the deck and burst on the console's windshield. Kyle rushed forward to open the hold and tug his rain jacket out of the top of his waterproof duffle. Win let off on the throttle, turned the boat to long enough to tug on his own jacket and a yellow hat that really did make him look like a throwback from a whaling ship now. Rain streamed off his dark face as he gripped the wheel and eased them into a slow lift and drop through the waves. Chaz let the rain beat on him, soaking through his T-shirt. But the rain picked up, beat down even harder on them, and a bolt of lightning ripped down through the rain and hit the nearest island. Chaz gave it up and scrambled and got his rain jacket, although he was already soaked to the skin when he put it on. The sheets of rain were coming at gale force, twisting in the wind to come from first one direction, then another.

Each drop that slammed against Kyle's face hurt as much as an ice crystal of sleet. The rain was warm, but it had a good deal of pent up force. He and Chaz huddled on the seat behind the console while Win stood and took the worst of the storm while keeping the boat pointed into the waves. Instead of passing quickly over, the storm hung over the boat, followed it along on its course, and kept their heads bowed. The skin of Kyle's face was tingling when the rain finally began to let up an hour and a half later. He could hear the sound of the bilge pump still running. But water sloshed around his ankles.

"Wow," Chaz said once the edge of the storm had slipped past. They could see the cloud drifting in toward the land, slanted streaks of gray beneath it. Then he looked around. "Where the hell are we?"

Win was frowning too. "Doesn't matter. This isn't that big a piece of the ocean that we can't get back. This isn't where we caught all the 'cuda before, but what say we give it a run or two along those rocky islands." He nodded toward a joined pair of mostly rock islands that jutted up, one end like a small diamondhead, the other more like the spine of some huge rocky animal. Bits of sea grape, copal, sapodilla, and saltwater palmetto had rough toeholds on the rock.

Chaz grabbed for his trolling rig, a Fin-Nor dual gear Ahab reel with eight hundred yards of sixty-pound test on a matching big game Fin-Nor rod with titanium rollers. It was an elephant gun compared to the fly-casting rig Kyle had brought. But Chaz had accounted for most of the barracuda caught so far. He and Win agreed that the fly rig Kyle used took too much time.

They all tugged off their rain gear and spread the jackets in the boat to dry, clipping them to the rod racks so they would not blow out of the boat during the trolling. Win turned the boat into a parallel course along the islands while Chaz clipped his steel leader onto a one-ounce flat-sided yellow jig with a tip of cut ballyhoo. He dropped the lure in the water and ran out line, then slipped the butt of the rod into one of the rocket-launcher rod holders.

"Too bad you didn't bring one like this," Chaz called to Kyle.

Kyle had the chance for a matching rig when Win had

bought them each their saltwater gear. Kyle had been drawn instead to the "Tarpon Buster" Fin-Nor anti-reverse fly reel that now held four-hundred yards of Dacron thirty-pound test line with an eight-foot Fin-Nor 13-weight blue-water fly rod. Same company, different spin on the game, Kyle thought. He would get his chance when they got to the sharks.

A third of the way into the first pass Chaz's rod bent suddenly, the line slicing into the water. The reel's drag screeched as line ripped out, heading out toward deeper water.

"Fish on," he called, and grabbed for the rod.

He had the rod butt against his stomach and clutched it above the reel with his left hand, lifting and cranking line back in by the time Win got the boat slowed. Win had to keep the boat in gear so they would not drift in toward the island.

Chaz horsed the barracuda toward the boat, close enough for Kyle to see the silver streak of the fish's side. But, as soon as it saw the boat it made another surging run. Kyle watched the rod throb in Chaz's hands as the reel's drag screamed. He caught the expression on Chaz's face, watched the determined stare shift to a smile as the line started coming back in as he cranked. This time, when he reeled the fish close, Kyle reached for the gaff and bent over the gunwale and lifted the three-and-a-half-foot 'cuda onto the deck.

Win glanced down at the barracuda and grinned. It lay like a poured bar of molten silver, all muscle and long teeth sharp enough to slice a tough parrotfish in half like a sushi knife going through raw tuna. Chaz grabbed for the small club-sized "no-alibi" aluminum bat and hit the 'cuda three crisp blows on the back of the head. It shivered and died.

Win turned away and was reaching for the boat's starter key when Kyle said, "Wait a minute. Give me a shot here on the drift."

Win turned to him, surprised, but pleased.

Kyle had already pulled his fly rod from the rack and now fit it together. The boat was in a drift that looked like the breeze and current would take it past the lower tip of the island. Kyle had spotted a long narrow shadow that flicked a ray of silver his way for the barest part of a second before looking like a sunken log again.

He still had one of the flies he had tied for shark at the end of the steel leader end of the tippet. It would do—a red-collar of thick marabou ahead of a tail of full-bodied red dyed rabbit fur in a five-inch long strip on a 4/0 Gamakatsu hook. He started the line out in a couple of false casts and shot out eighty feet of the weight-forward line, dropping the fly just where he wanted, bouncing it off the rocky tip of the island, letting it flutter into the water. He started stripping the line in with short rapid jerks. Kyle had barely moved the fly three feet when he felt the savage strike jar all the way up to his shoulder. He rocked back, lifting the eight-foot rod into a hard hook set, making sure the hook sank into that tough jaw. Then he had his hands busy.

This 'cuda felt bigger than any of the others he had hooked. It was stripping out flyline far too fast for Kyle to palm the reel and add drag. But he wanted to get it to the boat as quickly as possible to belie Chaz's beefing that using the fly rod took too long. When he tried to horse the fish toward the boat, it made a surge and stripped out fifty more yards of line. He dropped the line he held in his fingers before it could cut the flesh to the bone. Getting a flesh cut out on the saltwater was one of the last things he wanted to do.

When the 'cuda began to slow its run, Kyle lifted up on the rod and slammed a hand onto the drag on the outside of the reel at the same time. He could feel the fish's head snap around and the long body do a quick tumble underwater. Then the line shifted direction and he began to reel line back in as quick as he could. The huge silver bullet of a head shot straight up out of the water, then the long body after it, surging in a leap, making a twisting flop as the fish hit the water again and made a new sounding dive that caused Kyle's reel to sing. He glanced at Chaz and Win in time to see their expressions. The fish was well over five feet long, and Kyle was giving it a good go with his fly rig.

The 'cuda made a couple more runs, but Kyle gained on it each time. Finally the big fish turned on its side and let Kyle gain back all his line. Win was the one to sink the gaff this time. He and Chaz both had to lift to get the fish onto the deck, where Chaz finished it off with the club.

Win looked down at the two fish laying on the deck, then up at the boys. "Now we have fresh chum for the sharks," he said.

Kyle looked up at the drift of the boat. It had gone past

the island and had turned sideways to the waves, was troughing between the waves, then lifting on the next set. A few vegetation covered islands lay low across the far horizon. To the west, a cloudbank obscured the distant Maya Mountains, taking away the last hint of where they and the boat were.

"THEN YOU WON'T do it?" Margo Castle leaned forward in her chair, still wearing the dress she had worn during the wedding. Her hair was up in the rigid blond perfection she had altered little for the event, but her face had the pinched intensity it could get when she was very focused and determined. A vein stuck out along her neck and throbbed, and her skin was a pale flush of pink and darker pink.

"Impossible." The young Belize Navy lieutenant's diplomatic skills had been exhausted twenty minutes ago and the damn woman would not leave. Lt. Marc Ruiz had smooth and perfect skin the color of a coconut's inner hard shell. He was part mestizo and part Maya, a native-born Belizean who had climbed to an enviable social position for a man of thirty-two. His office was small and cluttered with papers, which represented a lot of work he should be getting done. "They should have taken a ship-to-shore radio with them, madam. That is the best practice."

"But they're after sharks."

"We also discourage that. But we cannot arrest them for that just yet." There was a twinge of accent to his voice, so that yet sounded faintly like "jet." But he was very proud of his English. It was what had helped him land his cushy spot in Belize, that and his usual good patience with the tourists. But he was very close to tossing this one out on her ear.

"All I'm asking you to do is find my husband and boys and bring them back here."

"And I been telling you that we cannot do that. Not unless they are missing."

"They are."

"Only since early this afternoon, you say."

He had been off to college in America when Belize split from Guatemala in the early 1990s, and it was there that he met young college girls he called "piranha women." He could tell that Margo had once been one, but was now the fully mature and an even more dangerous model, one who has had a tiny taste of power. He thought he had come home to Belize at the most opportunistic time, but then there were these occasional strains on his diplomatic skills.

"I thought this was a civilized country."

"Oh, it is, lady. You don't know this, but it is. You see the product before you now, though you cannot tell, can you?"

"Well, I can tell you that this is the last time I come to your stinking little country."

"*Bueno,*" he said, his famous patience completely exhausted.

THE BOAT BOBBED in the choppy green waves and drifted slowly to port. Kyle and Chaz wrestled with the two dead 'cudas until they were pressed against the nearest gunwale beneath the rod rack and were as out of the way as they could be for the moment.

"Don't worry about our location just yet," Win said. "Any fool could find his way back from here, even without that damned Boose being along."

Kyle was bent over the stern beside the motor and was washing some of the blood and barracuda slime from his hands. He looked back across the island-dotted expanse of water. All the storm clouds he could see were the small drifting kind that put down spots of rain and moved on. But on the far horizon he could see a few more of the big thunderhead cumulonimbus clouds stacking up. They should have rented the ship-to-shore radio as the man at the boat rental office suggested. But Win had insisted against that.

"I want to be sure you two understand the ground rules," Win said. "You both will have a chance at a shark, but you have to get the shark into the boat, same as the 'cudas. Understand?"

Chaz nodded with his characteristic eagerness. It took all Kyle had not to frown or shake his head.

"The word shark comes from the German word *schurke*, which means a scoundrel. That's the kind of blood line I want in charge of Camelot Hills and the Castle estate. Am I being as clear as I can here?" Win's stare moved back and forth between them.

Kyle thought the glitter in his father's eyes did not come from the harsh sun, but from some other driving bit of madness. There was a lot Kyle wanted to say, but it was all useless. He looked at Chaz, saw the same glitter in his eyes.

Win fired up the boat and headed toward the nearest clump of larger islands, looking for the kind of flats where sharks liked to come up and feed, where the boys could sight fish after them.

Kyle glanced at his watch. The wedding reception would be long over by now, and Maggie would be on her honeymoon in beautiful tropical Belize. She was now Mrs. Howard Julius Upwood. Kyle envied Maggie's not having to care any longer about what happened at the Castle estate. Howie was a bookish young man who wanted to do something "in the arts." His family's money came from his father's work as a venture capitalist in the early boom days of the high tech explosion. As far as Kyle knew, Howie lived off an allowance from a trust fund and had never worked a day in his life. Howie was a nice enough guy, though he could be a little vapid in a conversation that went into any detail. He could imagine Howie being asked along on this expedition and politely declining, worried that he might break a fingernail, or something.

The boat rocked through the waves until Chaz jumped up to stand beside Win and point toward a more shallow set of flats that formed between three close islands. Kyle could see a dark line, like a black log against the lighter sand and pale turtle grass. A tip of fin and then a swirl of dark tail showed above the water, the tail too short to be a thresher shark. But it was something feeding. The head jerked back and forth now as the boat veered closer to the flats and slowed. Chaz was already reaching for his big rod.

The water beneath the boat was still ten to twelve feet deep when Win turned off the motor. The wind started the drift that would take the boat in a sweep past the spot where they could see the active shark feeding.

Chaz cut the jig and its metal leader off the end of his line and tied on a fifty-pound test barrel swivel, a six-foot section of one-hundred-pound test monofilament for shock leader. He slipped on a one-ounce egg sinker, then tied an Albright knot onto a fifteen-inch length of fifty-pound test piano wire fastened to a 10/0 hook. He cut a chuck of barracuda from near the tail of one of the fish and put the dark red chunk of meat and silver bit of skin on the hook. He moved up in the bow of the boat and waited on the drift to take them closer.

He waited until they were close enough for Kyle to make out the wide hammer-shaped head from the back of the boat. Big eyes out on each far end flicked toward the boat as the shark swirled in tight circles, an indication of a feeding mood. It was at least eight feet long, perhaps two hundred pounds of tough fighting fish. Chaz cast and the sinker hit the water and made as much noise as a duck landing sideways. The shark snapped in an abrupt turn and shot away into the deeper water.

Chaz reeled in and turned back to Win and Kyle with a scowl.

"I thought we'd need the chum," Win said.

Chaz sat down in the bow while Win eased through a gap in the coral, a big piece of brain coral on the left, jagged broken pieces sticking up on the right. The boat just made it through, then the water was deeper again, five to six feet in a smooth flat covered with low underwater turtle grass and occasional dark pockets. Win eased the boat to a spot just inside the jaws of a cut that led into the flats from the far side. The waves were pushing small bits of coconut fronds and mangrove seeds through the gap. But the boat sat in the lee, the water nearly still around it. Kyle dropped the anchor in at Win's signal, and the boat swung around and took a position.

Once they were in place, they butterfly-filleted one of the barracudas, leaving the fillets hanging onto the body. Win tied the 'cuda's tail to a scrap of spare anchor rope and they hung the fish out into the water. Kyle watched an oily and bloody chum slick begin to spread from the boat.

Jellyfish floated past in thick clumps. On the bottom there were sea cucumbers, an orange or brown starfish here and there, and piles of lighter sand in the twisted shape of worms. Two small purple and yellow wrasses came up to investigate the chum barracuda, but shot off as soon as Kyle bent closer to look at them. The sun beat down on the boat. Kyle dug into his bag and took out a tube of sunscreen lotion. He rubbed it on his face and neck, then held out the tube to Chaz and Win. They both shook their heads.

They sat in the heat and waited, a light breeze lifting through the gap every now and then. Kyle watched needle-fish move along the edge of red mangroves hanging down into the water. He could hear the distant call of gulls. When the boat swung out on its pivot, he could see out onto the darker water where terns were diving at baitfish.

After a half hour of watching Chaz stare at his line, Kyle eased himself to the deck and leaned his back against the gunwale. As soon as he did, he heard Chaz gasp. There was a huge splash beside the boat. Kyle jumped to his feet, saw the rings of a wake where something big had jumped out of the water and back in. "What was that?"

"Manta ray," Chaz said. "Had to be six feet across."

Kyle had heard that they sometimes jump to shake off the parasites that cling to them.

Chaz was looking off in the direction the manta had gone. Kyle looked at Chaz's rod and saw the line give a jerk and lift. "Chaz."

Chaz spun and grabbed the rod out of the rod holder. Line was ripping out. Kyle saw the big mottled back of the tiger shark lift to the surface just as Chaz set the hook. He saw the rod shake left then right in Chaz's hands as the big head shook, then the rod snapped up and Chaz flew backwards across the deck and slammed into the far gunwale. He bounced off and slammed his rod against the gunwale, then stopped to make sure the rod was okay. When he saw it was, he reeled in the line, swung up the end, and looked at the bent hook. "That was one big shark," was all he could say.

"Bigger than the one behind you," Kyle said. "But this one's coming our way instead of going away." He grabbed for his fly rod.

Chaz rushed to his tackle bag and dug for a new hook. Kyle was already casting. He could see the sleek gray body and the black tips on the caudal and dorsal fins. It was a black tip shark, a kind of shark Kyle knew he never wanted to see when he was swimming.

Kyle's first cast overshot the fish, but the light splash of his fly did not send it scooting. It was still making a "V" in the water as it headed toward the filleted barracuda. Kyle lifted his rod and brought his stiff forearm forward. It was like hitting a wall. He looked back and saw that Chaz had put his thick fiberglass rod in front of the fly rod. All of Kyle's extended backcast line shot forward and tied itself in a huge knot around the upper third of the fly rod. Chaz lowered his own rod and swung his freshly baited hook out into the water. It landed with a small plop. The shark swirled toward it, grabbed at the bait. Chaz set the hook as soon as he saw the mouth close.

Kyle did not watch Chaz fight the fish. He saw Win's suppressed grin, then Kyle was bent on the far side of the boat straightening out leader from line and getting the godawful tangle off the end of his rod. Chaz fought the fish for almost an hour. If they had been on open water, or if the shark had been bigger, Win would have pulled anchor and followed the fish until it was tired. As it was, the fish was finally letting itself be pulled to the side of the boat just as Kyle had his line reeled back into place and was stowing the rod. He felt the warm flush of anger rippling up the sides of his neck. But Win was focused on the fish. It lay on its side, exhausted as Chaz drew it to the side of the boat. It was a small shark, eighty pounds or so, and it had given its all in the fight, had nothing left.

Chaz held the rod with one hand and grabbed for the flying gaff. He cleated off the end of the rope on the nearest cleat on his gunwale, slipped the flying gaff's hook into the shark's mouth, and yanked. The shark was so tired it barely surged against the gaff's hook. The flying gaff had twenty feet of rope attached to the gaff hook, but Chaz did not need to count on that this time. He tossed the gaff handle onto the deck and pulled at the rope. Kyle watched his back strain as the shark's head lifted to the top of the gunwale.

"We shouldn't put a live shark in the boat," Kyle said. Then he remembered his father's terms. He went to that side and reached down and grabbed the shark just in front of its tail, where it was smallest. He lifted and the whole shark slid over the edge of the gunwale and flopped hard onto the deck. Kyle skipped away, knew what a shark, even a tired one, could do.

Win stood near the stern with his arms folded, looking on. Kyle thought he looked prouder than he should.

Then the boat gave a jerk.

"What the hell?" Win spun, saw two nurse sharks fighting each other to suck the fillets off the chum barracuda. He grabbed at the rope, but was too late. When he hauled it up all he had was a head, the tail, and the 'cuda's spine. The nurse sharks shot off, two brown streaks, each making a "V" in the water.

Kyle took out his filleting knife and went over and cut butterfly fillets in the other barracuda. He tied its tail to the chum rope, dropped the blood-rimmed meat and silver skin of the carcass into the water, and avoided making eye contact with Chaz while he did.

Chaz was bent down by the shark's mouth, tugging at the hook that protruded from the bloody corner of its mouth while he held the small aluminum bat against the shark's nose. Kyle took his fly rod out of the rack and climbed up on the seat behind the console to have a look around with his small field glasses. He heard the scuffle below in time to look down and see the shark's lips pull back and the teeth and gums rocket forward and click as they clamped onto the bat handle. Chaz's right hand shot back and he got the left out just ahead of the click of teeth. The shark's head jerked left and right in a tearing motion.

Chaz scurried back on his knees away from the head. The bloodshot eyes glared at him, the mouth clamped tight on the bat, on what could have been Chaz's hand if he had been a second slower. Chaz was panting and his eyes were wide as he spun to look at Win.

"I've heard they'll do that," Kyle said, keeping his voice matter of fact. He lowered the binoculars and gave Chaz an unflinching stare.

Chaz—always a bit slow with a snappy comeback— was not able to speak at first. But he finally took a long shaky breath and managed, "Mine's still a lot bigger than yours."

"I just spotted mine," Kyle said. "All I have to do is go bring it in." He went to the stern and untied the diving ladder and let the lower rungs fold out to flop down into the water. The water was clear beneath the boat. He could see the current bending the turtle grass. The same two small purple and yellow wrasses flitted between the blades of grass. Jellyfish bobbed by steadily.

Kyle kicked off his deck shoes and took a pair of reef walkers out of his bag and slipped them on.

"What all do you have in that bag?" Chaz said. "You think you lugged along enough stuff for a half day of fishing?"

"You just never know," Kyle said, already climbing down into the water.

It was colder than he expected, and deeper. What had looked only two feet deep from the deck was up to his lower chest by the time his feet were on the bottom. As the cold swept over his crotch he was more awake and alive than he had been all morning. Good, because the dark shadow he had seen moving was edging its way along the shallows toward the chum slick. Kyle took slow forced steps through the water that began to get more shallow. He dodged the steady flow of jellyfish that spun by in the current. He did not like the idea of being in the same water as a hooked shark, or an unhooked one, but he could not risk being sabotaged again by Chaz either.

As he got closer to the mangroves the water became more shallow. He eased out around a stand where the mangroves shoved their red stems and air roots down into the water to form a small point. Ahead he could see the shadow he had spotted from the boat. He was close enough now to see the pointed sweep of the dark dorsal fin, then the blunt wide head as the black shark shimmied cautiously through the shallows toward the oily sheen of the chum slick coming from the boat.

The water was clear enough in the shallows Kyle knew he would have to cast in bonefish fashion, no more than a forty- or fifty-foot cast with a feather of a presentation. He stalked closer to the fish, the water just below his knees now. The shark seemed to be scouting the edges of the mangroves, knowing the tendency of even the largest barracudas to lurk back in the shallows where they could dart out for easy pickings.

Kyle waited until the thick dark body turned its wide hammer of a nose into a small cove before he stood out from where he hid and started his cast. He made two false casts and then let the line lay straight out, putting the fly just past the shark. The fly was still fluttering down through the water when the shark turned back toward the scent of the chum. Kyle made his first strip in of line. It moved the fly in a tantalizing twitch right in front of the shark's face. The shark surged and Kyle gave another strip, but the shark was too quick, its mouth closed over the fly and Kyle set the hook.

The second the hammerhead felt the twitch of steel in its mouth it shot straight up out of the water in an airborne surge that let Kyle confirm it was at least twice as big as Chaz's catch.

The first bursting run of the shark went straight across the length of the flats until half the line on Kyle's reel was gone. He had experienced great bonefish runs before, but never anything like this. He could not tell if his knees were shaking because the water was cool or if it was caused by the shark. But as soon as the hook was set he started back toward the boat.

When he feared that the shark would shoot out past the far reef out into the deeper water, he was forced to risk tightening the drag on the fish and lifting his rod back hard. The rod bent, took the head shaking of the big fish, then the fish turned, started back toward Kyle. He did not know where he had the fish hooked, but there must be enough sting to it to control the fish. But he was not sure he wanted it coming at him. He reeled in line as fast as he could, keeping tension on the fish. It circled wide now through the flats. Kyle looked up. He was halfway back to the boat. He could see Win and Chaz standing together in the bow, watching the shark fight.

The shark suddenly snapped toward the center of the flats, a "V" in the water marking its rush, then it shot out of the water again making an arching jump like a billfish. It landed with a flat splash on its side, shot off again as soon as it was underwater, ripping line back off Kyle's reel.

Kyle had sloshed to within six feet of the back of the boat. The water came to the middle of his thighs and made rushing hard, but he surged the rest of the way to the ladder and clambered up it while keeping a tight line on the shark.

He stood dripping on the deck. As soon as the shark neared a cut heading out of the flats, Kyle pulled back on his rod and tightened down the drag again. The shark turned and headed back directly toward the boat.

Kyle frantically reeled in line and moved to the front of the boat, nudged Chaz to the side when he would not give ground. Chaz tried to step back into Kyle, but Win reached out and grabbed Chaz by the shoulder and jerked him back to the middle of the boat. Kyle stepped up onto the bow and reeled.

The hammerhead tried an abrupt left, then shifted with a head shake to the right. Kyle kept reeling and gaining line. Then the shark spun in a complete circle, seemed to take a new bearing, and raced as fast as it could right at the boat.

Kyle reeled in line as quickly as he was able, but there was still a bit of slack in the line. That did not seem to matter to the fish. The hook was set well and it did not deter from its new plan. Water swelled up on both sides in the shallows and it flew right toward the boat and smacked its head directly against the port bow. Kyle rocked back on his feet, but kept his balance. I once surfed a bit, he told himself, and felt foolish for thinking it. The shark whirled and rammed the boat again, trying to bite at it with its teeth.

But the blows stunned the shark as much as the three men in the boat. Kyle was able to reel the fish up to the side of the boat, where it rocked to its side, the big eye on the end of its hammer head looking up blank into the sky.

Kyle looked at Win, who shrugged. He turned and looked for the flying gaff, but Chaz had never gotten its hook free from his shark.

Kyle grabbed the other one-piece gaff and reached down to hook the mouth of his shark. He tried to lift, but it was too heavy. Neither Win nor Chaz stepped forward to help.

"It's got to be in the boat," Chaz chanted.

The shark gave a shake, seemed to be getting its wind back and if it did, it might take off in another run.

Kyle never hesitated. He cut his fly leader and jumped over the side of the boat. He was in the water to his knees beside the shark, its rough skin rubbing against him like a raspy file. He could lift the shark's head out of the water with the gaff only to have the wide black head flop back in again. The shark's tail swished and the gills began to open and close faster.

Desperate, Kyle dropped the gaff and put both arms under the shark's head, lifting it, dragging the fish toward the stern. The movement only seemed to help the shark revive. It gave a twist, snapped back at him. But he fended off the bite by grabbing the beveled end of the shark's nose hammer and pushing. Then he tried to tug the fish to the boat again by hand. But the shark had some life back now. It thrashed in his hands, its mouth grabbing and snatching at water, barely missing Kyle. Arms came down from the side of the boat and Kyle felt himself lifted up and away from the fish just as the shark spun loose from his grip and would have got him. Win and Chaz hoisted him up over the gunwale and dropped him to the deck. Kyle wanted to rise, to dive back in, but he had used everything he had. He lay there, like one of the caught fish, and looked at his raw forearms and the blue sky rocking above the boat. He heard Chaz say, "There it goes."

All Kyle could think was what he had already known, "So this is how it is."

It seemed he lay there a long time getting back his breath and any energy. He saw his father's face bent over him, but there was no expression. When Kyle did turn his head he could look across the deck and see part of Chaz's shark laying on the far side, its skin drying and getting paler.

He was able to sit up as Chaz was pulling the anchor. Kyle heard Win turn the key. The thought that pressed to the front of his mind, after a long delayed struggle, was, "Why was the water knee deep when he got back to the boat when it had been chest deep when he left it?"

He was looking around and began to catch on as well.

Kyle pulled himself upright and looked around at the flats. He could see small mounds of islands now that had not been there before. "The tide," he said.

The sound of the key turning was followed by a click, then a shrill siren.

"What the hell?" Win tried again, got the same result.

"Trim the motor," Kyle called over to him.

Win levered the trim of the motor until it tilted up. This time it started, slow and sputtery, but it was going. He started forward until the bow bumped a sand dune.

"Okay, boys. Out of the boat. And get that fish out first. I need you in the water pulling on the tender."

Chaz and Kyle grabbed the shark, dead now, but still clamped onto the killing bat. They cut the gaff hook rope and heaved the shark over the side. Then they jumped off themselves. The boat rose in the water once at least four hundred pounds was off it.

Win steered toward the nearest cut, but the water got more shallow. He had to back and wait until Kyle and Chaz came around to tow on the boat's tender. Kyle could see the dead shark floating off into the maze of low mangroves.

They headed back toward the cut where they had entered the flats. Kyle was first in up to his chest, then to his waist. "I don't know," he called out.

Win finally killed the engine, trimmed the motor all the way up out of the water, and splashed in himself. The three of them tugged on the boat that swung around in the listless current.

Kyle tried not to think of the scene in the movie *African Queen* where Humphrey Bogart and Katharine Hepburn haul their boat along by its rope, but had no more success with that than when someone tells you not to think of a white bear.

The sun was lower in the sky when they had pulled the

boat all the way to the inside of the cut. The water was below Kyle's knees and he could see it rushing out between the coral gates of the cut.

"Faster," Win shouted. "We've only got…" And the boat ran aground. He strained, and both the boys put their shoulders to the rope, but it did not matter. The boat settled slowly onto its keel as the water ran on out through the gap.

All three of them climbed up into the boat as it rocked to its starboard. The rest of the water went out the cut and they were stranded high and dry.

"Well I'll be damned," Win said. He looked off in the direction he thought he might expect to see Margo. But all any of them could see was the islands getting bigger as the tide went all the way down to low tide.

"WHY ANYONE WOULD go to the Caribbean in June is beyond me," Esbeth said. She closed the door behind her and leaned on it. The last tour guests of the day were heading to their cars, each parked in whatever patch of shade they had been able to find in the parking lot. "It's hotter than an armadillo's armpit out there."

Esbeth let the air conditioning of the tasting room wash over her. Her eyes swept along the upper reaches of the high walls where the heads of deer, elk, and what looked like bighorn sheep were mounted—trophies of the young sahibs. Set up that high on the walls, she wondered who dusted their thick fur and racks of horns and antlers. The big dark glass eyes seemed to be looking back at her. She had known she was getting a little tired and punchy when she was asked about them by the last group and had told the folks, "Oh, just some road kill from around here."

Betty Sue was leaning against the counter where she had been chatting with Pearl. Well, that was different. But with the whole Castle tribe off to the wedding in Belize, Esbeth had gotten a better look at Betty Sue, who seemed to sparkle in their absence. She was a petite woman, barely five foot two, and seemed no bigger around than a pencil. Usually she moved quietly around the winery, or dragged. But in the past few days there had been a near skip to her steps. She smiled at Esbeth now.

"It's Miss Maggie's wedding," Pearl said. She looked up from where she had been busy adding to the day's wine and bric-a-brac sales. "They wanted something special."

"A lot of people think it's special to have their wedding here at the vineyard."

"Well, that wouldn't do for Maggie," Betty Sue said. "The way I heard it, she wanted the wedding to be on St. Lucia. But Margo got some kind of deal in Belize—a chance to save a few bucks."

Pearl said, "All those places sound pretty romantic to me."

"Thinking ahead toward if and when you get married again?" Esbeth asked her.

"I think I'm done with all that kind of foolishness after tangling with the likes of Rory Abrams."

"But you got little Collin out of it."

"Which just goes to show that something good always does come out of something bad, just like you're always saying," Pearl said.

"I know just what you mean," Betty Sue said.

Pearl said, "Yeah, Betty Sue met Bill here at the winery back when the Castles were starting it. They went to the same school but didn't link up till they were here. Betty Sue came as a lab technician, worked with Bill during some of those long evenings when they have to taste and test again and again until they get a batch just right."

"I thought Win did all of that as the winemaster," Esbeth said.

"He just takes all the credit," Pearl said. "He learned what he knows from them, then moved Betty Sue out of the lab and into the office."

Esbeth suspected that Pearl had got that from Betty Sue, who now felt a bit uncomfortable telling tales out of school. Betty Sue's voice lowered as she said, "I'm really better at the office things. I don't miss the lab work much."

Betty Sue was not the best liar Esbeth had ever heard. She was instead like a delicate bird fluttering onto a limb too tiny to hold her weight and flickering off into the wind almost as soon as she had landed. Change that someone else makes for you is never the same as that which you choose to make yourself. Esbeth knew that. Betty Sue's job put her in between the Castles and the rest of the help, the old rock and a harder place. The same was true of Bill, who managed Boose, along with his field hands and the other men. But Betty Sue held up well doing what not many other people would have had grace doing.

She was not as tiny as she seemed, either. Standing near her now, Esbeth realized Betty Sue was taller than she was herself, although so was the bulk of the adult population. Betty Sue just looked like such a tiny thing when she was next to her husband, Bill, who was not the giant he seemed either, except when around her. It was an odd chemistry for a marriage. Her smallness, yet so full of spunk and sparkle, was what made Bill seem meek and hulking, which he wasn't, except when the two graced each other with their presence.

Esbeth looked out across the vineyards where the tendrils above the canopy were swaying in the breeze and turning amber as the sun began to lower. "I wonder how the Castles are doing down there. Do you think they're getting along for once?"

"We sure are here," Pearl said. "Bill and Betty Sue Markley haven't been in such good spirits for a long time."

"Well, at least at a wedding maybe Win will let up on his two sons for a while," Esbeth said.

"I guess you don't know Win that well," Pearl said.

"Oh, and I meant to tell you, Esbeth, forget about paying for that missing case of wine," Betty Sue said.

Pearl's smooth, rounded face was twisted into a quick look of shocked outrage. She looked first at Betty Sue, then at Esbeth, and landed back on Betty Sue.

"She shouldn't have been the one anyhow. I'm in charge of the tasting room, no matter what," Pearl said. She turned to Esbeth. "Were you gonna pay for that case, even though we don't know…"

"Doesn't need discussion, ladies," Betty Sue said. "It's all straightened out."

"Did you find the case?" Pearl asked.

"Let's say I know about it now."

The door banged as Boose came through from the back.

Betty Sue did not stir from her lounge against the counter. She said to Esbeth, "Why don't you have half a glass of wine? You've had a day of it."

"Thanks, but I've got a long drive ahead of me. Folks of my years have to muster up their attention span for a long haul like that. You don't want me to be ready to nap during it." She thought a moment. "We're a fine bunch. You don't drink at all, do you, Pearl?"

Pearl said, "No. And Boose will have a beer when he gets home."

"Perhaps two," Boose said, and gave an unpracticed Popeye-like wink.

"Was that Bill Markley I heard whistling back there in the fermentation room today?" Esbeth asked.

"It sure enough was," Boose said. "Ever since the Castles took off you'd think Bill'd lost his possum and has to do his own grinning."

"It sure has gone a whole lot smoother with you and Bill running the place, Betty Sue," Pearl said.

Esbeth was watching Betty Sue, whose faced flushed to a light pink.

"Hell, my workers are darn near up to doing handsprings," Boose said. "No one's threatened to yank their green cards all week, and Bill caught Pablo grabbing a siesta and just smiled at him."

"You have no idea how hard Bill has it when the Castles are here," Betty Sue said. "He's had to do almost all the work since Win had his stroke, or whatever it was, and he gets no credit for it, and certainly not enough pay."

Esbeth caught herself wondering about the Castles,

what it was that made them think they were cut out of better stuff than other people.

Being an older woman never made Esbeth feel superior. At seventy-two she still felt the same way inside her head as she had when she was sixteen years old. She had just learned that her body did not always keep up with her the way she would like.

She looked around at the others in the room—Betty Sue, a different person when she was relaxed for a change; Pearl, shining on the half shell like the young girl she was; and Boose, grinning instead of looking like he wanted to bite someone.

It was Maggie who had mentioned poison. But it seemed to Esbeth that it was the whole Castle tribe who were slowly poisoning those who worked around them.

"Aren't they due back any day now?" Esbeth asked.

"I probably shouldn't say anything," Betty Sue said, a barely suppressed smile rippling across her face, "but I just got a telegram from Margo. They're staying on for a day or two more."

Pearl tilted her head. "Imagine that. Margo can't be pleased, spending money. Do you suppose the boys got caught up in having a bit of fun?"

"I hope they are," Esbeth said. "I hope they have such a good time they decide to stay an extra two weeks. It seems everyone here gets a lot out of their vacations."

"I hope for Miss Maggie's sake that she's getting the most out of this one," Boose said.

"Don't be crude," Pearl said, though she seemed to smile at the thought of a honeymoon.

"We can't all be off having our fun in the tropics," Boose added, "but if the rest of them Castles wanna stay a few more days, or a few more years, I say power to them."

Pearl said, "They're not so very bad when they're around."

"I don't know," Betty Sue said.

Esbeth's eyes went back and forth between them, as if watching a Ping-Pong match.

"The only one to ever give me a really hard time was that Chaz," Pearl said.

"And if I ever…" Boose started to butt in.

"Don't say it," Pearl warned.

"I never said I'd kill him," Boose's voice got louder as he heated up. "I said I'd yank his tongue till it grabbed asshole, then I'd play him like a yo-yo."

He spun and stomped out of the tasting room, all stirred up and ready for business.

When the door closed behind him, Pearl gave a delicate little shudder and said, "Folks think he just has a colorful way of talking, but I've seen him try to do that to someone."

"Well, you don't need to worry, Pearl." Betty Sue still watched the door where Boose had stormed out. "If anything ever happens to any of the Castles, we'll *all* be suspects."

FOUR

"I WANT YOU to call Margaret Castle's, I mean Upwood's, cabin again."

The desk clerk looked up. The smile oozed from his face when he saw Margo Castle standing there. She wore a tropical flowered outfit with toucans, hibiscus blooms, and lush jungle foliage in bright yellows, reds, and greens, but there was nothing festive about her expression. "I just did a few minutes ago. She said she didn't want to be disturbed."

"I'm her mother."

"She mentioned that." He looked at her, his lips pressed together on his lean dark face, no longer able to work his way back to his everyday desk man's smile.

Margo spun and stalked off. The worst of it was that there was no one to talk to. Maggie stiff-arming her, and the boys and Win missing. She had pestered the Navy officer again until he had said, "I don't know who you are where you live, lady. But you're not that here, let me assure you."

She looked up, found herself by the pool. She could see Bea and Chaz's kids over playing in the shallow end. That's not what she wanted. She did not even want to call Cassie's room to talk with her about Kyle being missing. But there was a bar.

She went over and sat down on an empty stool. There were only two other customers at the bougainvillea-covered poolside watering hole. The bartender was smiling when he came over. "What'll it be?"

"Piña colada," she said. "And keep them coming."

Maurice, the bartender, smiled again, which was somehow a scrap of comfort in her present mood.

An hour and three more drinks later, she felt tired and lay her head down on the bar's cool teak wood top. As her eyes closed, she could see Maurice coming toward her, and she tried to smile. After all, he was the only real friend she had in the whole world.

WIN SAT IN a slumped tilt on the seat behind the boat's console. The boat sat with dry hull, tilting to its starboard. The flats area where they had fished was reduced to low wide-scattered puddles and trickling streams that wove through the moist sprawl of mud and sand.

"No one thought to bring anything to drink, did they," Win snapped.

"Water," Kyle said. He was rubbing on more sunblock. This time Chaz reached out when Kyle offered the tube.

"You know what I mean," Win said.

Kyle glanced at him, tried to get a fix on this man who had passed as his father for all these years. The distant storm clouds on the horizon seemed to be reflected in Win's eyes; something was twisting inside him like a wet rawhide knot drying in the sun.

Kyle walked back to the stern that dipped down where it had settled into the groove of the channel. Crabs were climbing out of holes and scuttling across the open expanses of what had once been water-covered flats. The sun beat down on the boat and them, even though it was fading as it became late afternoon. Kyle glanced at his watch. He doubted if they would have water enough to float their way out of here until after dark. When he turned his head and looked the other way he could see brown pelicans diving for small fish out in open water just beyond their reach. But Kyle, Win, and Chaz could not very well pick up the boat and carry it out to the open water.

"Tides. Why didn't any of us think of that?" Win said.

Kyle nearly said that Boose would have, but he did not like the look on his father's face. Though it was far from the best time, he did say, "Where do we stand on this contest?"

"I think you know the answer to that. Chaz got his shark into the boat. That's how it worked."

"But you've got to listen to me." Kyle's voice began to betray him and waver.

"It's to run a winery, not a whinery," Win said. Chaz broke into a gloating grin.

Kyle could not bring himself to look at his father, even though it was the answer he had expected of him. He busied himself with stowing his fly rod. Then he looked at the scene of desolation around them. He still wore his reef walkers, so he climbed down the ladder and started off across the sand and mud toward the open water he could see ahead. As he went by the bow of the boat he could see stress marks where the shark had slammed into the boat, but the fiberglass was not cracked open, not that it mattered a whole lot with the boat sitting cocked and use-less on land.

He felt as bad as he had ever felt, but there was some-how no surprise to it. He had seen this coming. Win's mind had been made up some time ago, all the rest was window dressing leading to making sure Chaz was the big inheritor, not Kyle. It was funny; all his life Kyle had lived in the shadow of expectation of having the whole estate someday, but he could never fully picture it. He had not wished his parents dead, or longed for any of the power. Maybe that was what Win saw missing in him. It was hard to say.

Shells and sand dollars crunched beneath his steps. He skirted a pile of kelp against the side of a dune and stepped out onto coral where the waves lapped against the darker wet stone and skeletons of ages of coral past. An exposed red-orange starfish had a bare half inch of water over it where it clung in a small tide pool. The sun hit it and made it glow in a brighter color than Kyle had ever seen. He heard a flopping and saw a small blue parrotfish tossing on its side within a foot of deeper water. He eased down across the sharp coral until he could scoop up the fish and toss it into the water where it shot off like a small blue bul-let.

He should feel rage, but he felt a strange peace. He looked out across the lapping waves and tried to figure out why. Perhaps it all seemed more inevitable, something he had known but had been denying. Chaz was his father's fa-vorite, a hardball player like Win. He tried to picture what life would be like when they got back to the Texas estate, but could not get it in focus. Then he wondered what he was going to tell Cassie, or worse, what she was going to tell him.

THE SERVICE ELEVATOR DOOR opened and Marta, a house-keeping maid, saw Maurice wheeling a woman inside on an office chair with wheels. Marta moved her cart to the wall so Maurice would have room to wheel the woman in. The woman's blond head lolled to the side and she was lightly snoring. The woman was dressed in the usual tour-ist garb bought from the hotel gift shop at prices ten times what Marta would ever have to pay.

"*Que es,*" she said to Maurice.

"Bernardo's watching the bar for me while I make a de-livery," Maurice said. He glanced down at Margo Castle. "A little miscalculation on my part. I thought this one was good for the long distance. Turns out she was a sprinter. She musta been emotionally stressed or something."

Marta gave a small, delicate snort. "*Los ricos,*" she said.

KYLE LOOKED UP at the sound of a screech high above him. It was hard to tell how long he had been sitting out by the water, but it was lapping at his ankles. The tide had turned. High in the air an osprey was carrying off a small silver fish to where it would settle on one of the islands and have dinner.

The sun was lower in the sky, and the breeze against his face felt cooler. He bent to the saltwater and slapped some onto his face. It felt cool to his skin. Then he rose and sloshed back through the deeper puddles toward the boat. Kyle could see each wave lapping closer as the tide rose. In an hour or so they might have enough water to float out past the coral.

As he got closer to the boat he could see Win sitting upright behind the console, his face closer to the color of an angry brick than it should have been. He had stubbornly declined any sunblock, had sat the whole time glaring at the cut that led to the sea, as if their being stuck was someone else's fault.

Chaz's head appeared over the gunwale as Kyle walked around to the stern ladder.

Chaz tossed an empty Evian bottle out onto a small sand dune. Kyle stopped, turned, and went over to pick up the bottle. "We might need that," he said.

"For what?" Chaz's face was not as sun-burned as his father's, but he looked petulant, perhaps a bit triumphant, though Kyle told himself he might be reading that into the look.

Kyle climbed up into the boat. "We'd better put out an anchor. The tide's started in. We don't want to be bounced all over the place until we can start up and head out of here."

Win gave a flick of his hand toward the anchor, but did not say anything. Kyle figured he must be thinking of a glass of red wine, though in this heat he could not imagine anyone enjoying that.

They had to sit and wait into the edge of the dark of night for the water to get high enough. First, the boat rocked, then lifted and straightened, finally it rode its anchor line, swaying back and forth while the water filled up the flats.

Kyle looked over the low islands around them. They were mostly mangrove and other low scraps of vegetation—what the locals call "wet" cays. To the west, the sky layered into bands of purple and pink across the rounded edges of silver, then gold, clouds.

"Beautiful sunset," he said.

"Kyle."

"What, Dad?"

"Shut up."

When it was dark enough for Kyle to see the first of the stars, the boat sat high in the water and Win said, "Lift the anchor."

Kyle said, "Hadn't we better…"

"Lift the damn anchor."

Chaz hurried forward and tugged them to the anchor, then lifted it up into the bow.

Win turned the boat's key and the siren split the night in two.

He turned it again. Siren.

The engine would not start. He turned the key frantically, again and again. All they got was the sound of the warning siren that told them something was wrong. But they knew that.

"Stop it, Dad." Kyle was surprised to hear his own voice.

"What'd you say?"

"I said to give it a rest. Even the siren's starting to wear down. You're not helping by grinding on the key. It isn't going to start like that."

Win let go of the key he'd been twisting and spun toward Kyle.

"Let's take a look at it," Kyle said.

"And find what?"

"I don't know. I'm no whiz with motors. Let's hope it's something obvious."

Kyle went back to the motor. It was a big 200-horsepower engine. He had to feel around in the dark for the latch that released the cowling. When he found the sideways latch he pushed on it until it released. Then he eased the plastic covering off the motor and set it on the deck before turning back to the motor. Chaz came to stand beside him.

"Do you see anything?" Kyle asked.

"No. Nothing loose or leaking," Chaz said. He bent out to look back as far as he could. "But it's kind of hard to see in the dark. I'll bet that..."

"Don't you dare mention that name," Win snapped.

Before either of them could say Boose's name, Win turned the key again. The siren made both boys jump.

"Stop it, Dad. I mean it."

Win did not comment on Kyle's tone this time. But he let go of the key and walked up to the bow to watch the boat's slow progress.

Kyle shook his head and put the cover back on the motor. "We have to figure something out."

The boat was drifting, being pushed by the stiff night breeze toward the cut that led out of the flats. The ocean was a rippling layer of silver waves past the foam of the water pouring through the coral reef gates.

"We'll get out of here," Win finally said. "But God knows where the current and wind will take us."

He spun and gave a savage kick to the seat on the front side of the console.

"Careful, Dad, your heart."

"Let me worry about that."

"We could anchor and wait on help in the morning." Kyle noticed that Chaz was not saying anything while their father was in this mood.

"No. We drift."

When they were up to the reef, there was a tense moment or two when Kyle had to reach out with the boat's only small oar to push them away from the brain coral. Then they were suddenly through and the wind caught them with new vigor and the boat started to drift toward the north.

"Well, we're headed in the right direction at least," Chaz said at last.

The moon was the barest sliver in the sky. In spite of the dark sky and darker ocean water surrounding them, Kyle could see their faces clearly, though Win's was darker.

"What's going to happen when we get back to Texas?" he asked.

"I want Chaz to move over as assistant winemaster, start learning those ropes from me." He paused, "And you, Kyle, might was well take over as overall sales manager."

"What about Clive Abramson?"

"Screw Clive Abramson. We're talking about family here." Kyle supposed that went for Bill Markley too, who had been with the winery since Win had started it. Chaz had avoided asking about Bill's fate.

For a while it was silent in the boat. The sound of the waves should have been relaxing to Kyle, but he was thinking about how things would be when they got back to the estate—for that matter, when they got back to the hotel.

"I'm hungry," Chaz said after an hour of silence. He and Win both sat on the seat behind the console.

Kyle rose from the seat in front of the console and opened the bow hatch to dig in his bag. "I've got two Power Bars," he said.

He took them to the back. Chaz grabbed one of them.

"We should share," Kyle said.

Win took the bait knife and cut the remaining bar in two, gave half to Kyle, but did not say anything to Chaz who was wolfing down the bar he held. He tossed the glittering wrapper over the gunwale.

There was something barbaric to Chaz that Win was encouraging and bringing out. Kyle tried to feel anger but could not. He felt mortally sad.

In all his life Kyle had never had anything gnaw at him like this. He felt in part embarrassed that he had had such an easy life. It was a silver spoon shame he had never expected to deal with, but there it was, once every expectation he had lived with since he was a child had flown away.

He went back up in the bow, stretched out, and in spite of all that bothered him, was able to doze off.

Kyle woke to the sound of shouting. He opened his eyes, saw the spray of stars in the sky, bright as tiny spotlights. He could make out the constellation Gemini before he could figure what Win and Chaz were yelling about. He sat up, blinking and looking around. He saw the low wall of white froth toward which the boat was drifting at a fast clip.

The boat was rocking sideways in the waves as it headed toward the reef. Kyle climbed up on the seat and looked ahead. The dark shadow of an island lay ahead. In front of it, out fifty yards from a sandy beach that Kyle could see even from here, was the reef. He dropped back to the deck and grabbed for the small oar.

"We've got to turn the bow forward, steer the boat to the right, if we can," he shouted. "There's a gap in the reef."

Neither Win nor Chaz sprang into action. They stood and shouted as they watched the reef get closer. Kyle climbed out onto the bow as far as he could, reached out with the small oar, and began to turn the boat, at the same time pulling it as far to the right as he could. Bent over in an awkward and uncomfortable position, he stroked hard with the small oar, looked up ahead and saw the gap still a bit to the right. He bent his head back down and pulled at the water as hard as he could, stroke after stroke.

The white froth was suddenly all around him, he could not have seen anything if he did lift his head, so he kept stroking as the boat took a small bounce off a coral head, slid to its starboard, and shot through the gap with only a long slow scrape of coral against the fiberglass of the port side hull.

Kyle lifted himself up painfully into the bow, watched the boat settle into its sideways drift as they headed for the pale sandy shoreline that seem to zoom toward them. "Hit the trim," he called out.

Win rushed over to the console and flipped the toggle. There was still power enough to raise the motor. It whined up, the prop lifting up out of the low waves just as the rocking boat scraped on the sand for the first time.

The boat jarred when it hit, then settled. The next few waves lifted it farther up onto shore until the boat stopped. Chaz hopped out, then Win. The boat moved farther up onto the shore. Kyle stood, his legs braced against the tilt of the deck. He stretched and moved his extended tired arms. Then he eased to the landward starboard gunwale and hopped over onto the sand.

No-see-ums bit into his legs as soon as he was on the beach, hundreds of them, biting and irritating him all the way to his thighs. Mosquitoes whirled around his head, making the rest of him as miserable as they could.

"This place sucks in a huge way," Chaz said.

Aside from having an abnormal number of biting insects, Kyle could not yet see enough of the island to form any conclusion. There was no way of knowing how big the island was, if it had any fresh water, or if they could be easily found in the morning. But none of those questions would be answered until daylight. The edge of the beach rose into a small row of dunes, then faded into thick vegetation that was black with shadows of brush that rose into taller trees.

The sharp blades of grass that rose out of the dunes sliced at Kyle's feet. He turned back and climbed up into the boat. The mosquitoes followed him, but the no-see-ums stayed on the beach. He rubbed at his itching shins and calves and got out his rain jacket for a cover. The boat gave a final lurch or two as the last of the high tide took the boat up onto the beach as far as it could. Kyle sprawled across the front seat and tried to sleep.

He woke to the growing light and the sound of two great-tailed grackles fighting over what remained of a dead crab. His back was stiff as he creaked into an upright position and looked out over the lower gunwale at the beach. A row of shell scraps and kelp marked where the tide has stopped several feet up the beach from the boat. The dark grackles were still bouncing around, squaring off at each other, and squawking over the bit of crab. From his height in the boat he could see the yellow rain jacket spread in a hollow between dunes where Win had tucked in to sleep. Chaz lay in a hollow of the dunes even closer to the green of vegetation Kyle could see more clearly now. Low bushes of sea grape, palmetto, and other scrub plants led up to the mat of gumbo-limbo trees and coconut palms.

The gnawing hollow he felt in his stomach told him he needed to start looking around if they were going to survive. He opened his waterproof duffle and took out one of the two spare quarts of water he had brought. He took a small sip and put the bottle back. They would have to go easy on that until they found if there was freshwater on the island, something he doubted.

He climbed down from the boat just as Win and Chaz were nearing it. Chaz's face was blank, in a near pout. Win was frowning at the boat as if it had personally affronted him. "We're going to have another look at the motor," Win said.

"I can help if you want." Kyle shifted his weight from one foot to the other.

"No need, unless you know more than the last time you looked under the cowling."

It was sarcastic enough for Kyle not to answer. He watched them climb into the boat and wrestle the cover off the motor again. They both stared in at the jumble of colored wires and maze of motor parts, neither looking like he spotted anything obvious.

Kyle turned slowly away from them and took his first walk along the shore. High up along the shore, tangled in a pile of broken coral rocks, was a sixty-foot length of a ship's rope. It was made of bright blue and white nylon and was as big around as Kyle's waist. He kept his eye out for anything they could use, and the rope was not one of them.

His stomach drove him out into the shallows, where he found he could wade halfway out to the reef before he saw any sign of fish. He bent to the surface and cupped his hands like a scuba mask and looked down into the water. He could see only a small gobi hovering above a scrap of loose coral. In the distance he noticed a darting shadow or two of what could be a jack, a grunt, or a mutton snapper. He turned and started back toward the shore. Halfway in, he came across the exposed halves of closed pen shells sticking out from the sand. He bent and gathered as many as he could, took them to shore, and came back for more. When he waded back in with another double handful, he found Win and Chaz down from the boat and on the beach. The cover was back on the top of the motor, though neither of them mentioned it, and Kyle knew better than to ask. Chaz was prying open the pen shells as fast as he could and sucking out the small hinge muscles.

Kyle frowned at him. "There's a bed of them out there if you want to gather some."

"These will do," Chaz said, reaching for another.

Win's face was like a red blister in the growing morning light. He looked around at the small island. "Probably too small to be inhabited," he said.

"If it was," Kyle said, "we'd probably have heard the generator by now." He looked into the heart of the tiny jungle at the center of the island. "But there might be an old fishing camp or even a spring of freshwater. It's worth a look."

He dropped the rest of the shells onto the dwindling heap and started off toward the thick green wall. Win squatted and started opening shells too before Kyle was out of sight.

The sea grape and other plants had been beaten into a tight slanted mass of bristly green by the wind and salt. The slant tapered up to the edge of the trees. Kyle found a small natural path that cut through the scrub, but it dwindled away as he got to the thick knot of low gumbo-limbo limbs. He bent low and looked as far as he could into the shadows, and saw only spider webs and more branches. Kyle stood and skirted along the outside of the mass of green until he was able to ease around along the shoreline, sometimes having to climb out onto jagged rocks or step through low mangrove clumps. A small barracuda shot off into deeper water when his foot came down once. He looked out across the ocean on the other side of the island. The ring of reef followed around and closed off this side too, but it ran in closer to the shore. He could see the hulking shadows of the Maya Mountains off fifty miles to the west, but he could see no other boats.

The woods opened up into a grove of taller coconut trees and he eased through the thick growth of young coconut plants at the base of the taller trees. In as far as he could press, he found no spring or sign of a fisherman's camp. He clawed his way back out to the shore, his shirt soaked through with sweat, and continued on around the edge of the water until he came back within sight of the boat. He was hot and exhausted, but what he saw caused him to break into a run.

Chaz stood on the shore near the beached boat. Kyle's waterproof duffle lay on the sand and part of its contents was scattered across the beach. Win sat a few feet away, staring out across the water.

At a full run, Kyle came up to Chaz who was slowly lowering a nearly empty quart container of water. Chaz wore a sneer for only part of a second. Kyle never slowed. He hit Chaz with his fist low in the center of the chest with all he had. Chaz bent double and dropped to his knees. Kyle slid to a stop in the sand, a bit past Chaz. He spun and grabbed Chaz by his blond hair and snapped his head back. Chaz fell all the way back onto the sand, the bottle rolling from his fingers. Kyle jumped onto him, straddling him and began to hit Chaz with both his fists. Chaz lay gasping for breath, his head whipping to left and right with each blow.

Win yanked Kyle off Chaz and pulled him upright. Chaz lay gasping, his face pink with needing air and from the blows. Kyle spun to face Win.

Win opened his eyes wide and he took a step back. Kyle was panting and his face was flushed in anger.

"Careful," Win said. "That's the Castle heir there." He may have known all along it was the last thing he should have said.

Kyle took a step forward until his face was inches from Win's. He jabbed a finger at Win's face and shouted, spit flying with every word, "Then you keep him out of my stuff or you're going to bury your heir on this goddamned island. Do you hear me?" His shouting ended in a hysterical pitch.

Win nodded, slow at first. Then he stepped around Kyle and bent to see if Chaz had learned to breathe again. He had, but it was not perfect at first. His arms grabbed at nothing and his mouth opened and closed.

Kyle's own breathing was getting back to normal. As it did he found it hard not to smile. Chaz looked like a fish out of water. But the color was coming back to his face, so Kyle knew he would be all right. He had mixed feelings about that.

Kyle began to pick up his belongings and put them back in his bag.

"You could have killed him," Win said.

"And…" Kyle said. "What's your point?"

"You were holding out on us, had water you didn't tell us about."

Kyle finished putting everything back into the bag, including the empty bottle Chaz had drained. He moved over to his father and twisted his shoulder roughly around until Win's face looked up at his own. Win looked startled.

Kyle had to force himself to speak as slow as he could. "That asshole just drank half of our entire water supply. If we're out here more than a day, he will have killed both you and I. We have to ration everything. You tell him, when he's fit to talk to, that if he touches anything of mine again we'll be having him for our first decent meal."

He let go of his vise grip on his father's shoulder and spun away. Kyle picked up his bag and walked over to the shade of a tree that stretched out over the sand. He put the bag down and went to the boat for his fishing gear. With the fly rod together, he went to the shade, got out his fly book, and tied on a smaller deceiver pattern fly on a monofilament tippet. Even in the shade, with the breeze blowing, he could feel the heat of anger still rippling through his face. He glanced across the beach, saw the two of them close together talking.

For the first time in his life, he did not feel like a part of the Castle family. And for reasons he was not ready to sort through at the second, that felt more good than bad.

Kyle stood and looked out across the sun-washed ripple of waves. There was a distant cloud or two, but, so far, today was a lot more sunny than the previous day. That could go both ways. He would have preferred a cloudy day since he was fishing now to live.

He put on fresh sunblock and waded out into the water. It was only to his knees for a long time, then took an abrupt drop-off into deeper and cooler water. He began to cast, working his fly out as close to the reef as he could cast. It was fortunate he had brought the fly rod, because Chaz's heavyweight rig was worthless for this kind of fishing where it counted. But his hopes began to fade after what felt like a hundred casts, when his arm began to tire.

He finally had to reel up and walk back up to the beach. There was more of it now that the tide was low.

"Giving up?" Win called to him from the shade. Chaz sat beside him, and stared at Kyle, but said nothing.

"I'll go back out when the tide turns," Kyle said.

"Too bad we didn't keep Chaz's shark," Win said. "We could eat that."

"No we couldn't." Kyle had stopped halfway over to his own shady spot. "A shark stores its waste materials in its tissues. When a shark dies, urea and all the other fluids break down into ammonia. If you don't bleed a shark by cutting off its head or tail, which we didn't do, the meat will taste and smell bad."

"By God, you're a regular Robinson damn Crusoe," Win said. He came close to smiling.

Kyle was thinking of the old line that Robinson Crusoe was the only person ever to get his work done by Friday. But he did not have the energy or the sense of humor to share it right then. He walked on to his shade.

He plopped down and opened his bag. He took out the empty water bottle and the Evian bottle Chaz had tried to toss away earlier. Kyle took the full quart of water and divided it among all three bottles until they were equal. He took a small sip from his bottle, then carried the other two bottles over to Win and Chaz. They looked up at him without rising.

"By rights I should have split the water in half and given half of it to you, Dad. Whether you shared with Chaz or not would be up to you. As it is, here. This is the last of the water. Right now it's the most precious thing we have." He handed them each a bottle. Chaz grabbed his with a minimum of eye contact. One eye was swelling and there was a lump along his cheek. "Now why don't you two gather up some banana leaves, some coconut fiber, and what wood you can? I'm going out to catch fish, and if I catch any, there had better be an equal share saved for me. Am I clear?"

Win nodded. Chaz looked away.

"Did you say bananas?" Win asked.

"None are as big as my little finger yet," Kyle said. "I thought the same thing at first."

Kyle waded back out through the waves. The water was cool, but no longer refreshing. He felt a tired ache to the center of his bones. Whether it was from hunger, thirst, or disappointment in his family he could not tell.

He lifted the rod and made his first cast. It would be the first of many he would make without catching anything. He felt a couple of small ticks as he got closer to the gap in the coral, the water rising all the time as the tide came in. But whatever hit at the fly missed.

Kyle stopped for a while and rested his arm. He could look back and see Win and Chaz moving around on the beach. Now that he had shot off his own mouth he did not want to go back in until he caught something.

The water was up over his waist now. He lifted the rod and made another cast. The fly was just settling through the water this time when the rod tip snapped down in a tug and he set the hook out with a long pull on the line with his left hand and a simultaneous lift of the rod with his right arm. The live fish on the end of the line felt like hope itself. He reeled in the slack and then the fish. It was a one-pound yellowtail. He grabbed it with his left hand, low on the belly to avoid the razor-edged gill covers, and carried it to the shore.

Chaz ran over to get it while Kyle waded back into the water. He was able to add two small barracudas to the catch before he caught another yellowtail. When he brought the last fish in, he flopped onto the sand. His arm felt ready to fall off.

Chaz scooped up the last fish and cleaned it by slitting the stomach and pulling out the entrails. He left the head, tail, and scales on the fish, wrapped it in one of the small banana leaves and put it into the pit where the fire was going. Win brushed sand over the top of the folded leaves. Smoke filtered up through the sand, along with the smell of roasting fish.

"You sure those 'cuda are okay to eat?" he asked Kyle.

"It's just the big ones get ciguatoxic," Chaz said before Kyle could answer. "Comes from eating fish that eat the red coral."

Kyle could have argued a bit with that, but it was not worth the bother.

Win reached over to a pile of coconuts they had gathered while Kyle fished. They had managed to tear the green husk off one and break open the inner brown shell. The milk was gone, but big chunks of white meat still clung to the inside.

Kyle went and got his knife, took a small sip of water, then came back and busied himself with prying out chunks while the fish cooked. Neither Win nor Chaz mentioned the small scuffle earlier.

When the fish were done, Kyle took one of the small barracuda and tore the flesh off with his knife and ate it while it was still steaming. Even with no spices, it was some of the best fish he had ever eaten. All of them bent over their unfolded leaves, eating like three cavemen, almost made Kyle laugh. But he said instead, "I haven't seen anything like a boat all day. How about either of you?"

They shook their heads. "Or a plane or 'copter," Chaz muttered.

Kyle glanced over at the boat. But his eyes lifted and caught the sky instead. "Uh oh."

"What?" Win looked up, then saw it too. A line of dark clouds was bearing down on the island, as if lifting up from the far horizon like a curtain. They could already see the gray slanted lines beneath the clouds, and here and there a spearing crack of lightning.

This was not one of those refreshing little showers common to June. This was as close to a tropical storm as the islands get before early hurricane season in the Fall.

Kyle bolted down a big piece of fish and put the rest down on the ground. Still chewing, he ran for the boat and climbed up in it. He tossed the anchor out from the bow and then got out the spare anchor rope, another hundred feet of it. He jumped over the gunwale down onto the sand. The first drops of rain were beginning to hit the sand hard, sending up small puffs of dust in the sand above the high tide line. He tied the end of the spare line to the anchor and ran all the way up to the woods, forced his way in until he reached the big bole of a tree, stickers scratching him and rain starting to come down harder as he tied the rope around the trunk. Then he scrambled for what had been his bit of shade and tugged on his rain jacket. The rain was already coming down in sheets of silver needles. He huddled close to the tree, with his back to it. He was wet beneath the rain jacket, looking out at all the freshwater pouring down when it hit him. He took his rain jacket off and went out into the downpour to cut sticks, two long ones and a couple of shorter ones. He pulled down a long length of vine and cut it into shorter lengths. He knew the vine was not from a poisonous ivy, but he had seen the mottled black-on-gray bark of poisonwood in the small woods.

The rain was coming down so hard it made seeing difficult. Thunder rippled through the storm and lightning hit all around them. He staked his jacket out so it formed a scoop and watched the rain fill it. Then he tapered the bottom so it led to the neck of his water jug.

While the jug was filling he dashed through the downpour and lightning over to the tree where Win and Chaz huddled together. He waved them to follow him. They reluctantly got to their feet and did. He showed them what he had done with his water jug, then he pointed the way to the woods. They turned and went that way to cut themselves sticks and bits of vine.

He sat and watched his jug until it was full, then he drank as much as he could before letting it fill again. Then screwed the cap back on and put the jug against the tree. It was still raining and getting darker as he took his jacket off the sticks and turned to his side on the wet sand, fluffed up a soggy lump of it, and lay down, pulling the jacket over him like a blanket. He didn't expect to be able to sleep. But he dozed off while still considering their dilemma.

KYLE FELT A SHARP PAIN on his nose and woke, snapped upright with a hermit crab dangling from his face, one pincher clamped to a nostril, its whelk shell swinging back and forth, bumping into his lips. He reached up and pulled at it, had to yank twice to get it to let go. Then he put it down on the sand beside him and looked around. It scuttled away. The sky was just beginning to get light. He brushed sand off himself as much as he could, but it seemed to have gotten into his hair and every other crack and crevasse of him. There were mosquito bites too. He was scratching at them when he heard Win shouting and looked down the beach that way.

His father had jumped to his feet, and now threw his own rain jacket out across a dune. Chaz was sitting up slowly from between two nearby dunes. Kyle could make out the word "scorpion." There were apparently worse ways to wake up other than having a hermit crab giving you a nose pick.

He looked over to the boat. It was a couple of feet higher onto the beach and twisted at a new angle. Win's continued shouting turned Kyle's head again. His father was kicking the dunes, breaking limbs, stomping across the sand. The only time Kyle had ever seen anything like it had been on a nature film about the great apes.

Kyle got up slowly, hesitated before he went over to the other two. Win rushed to the edge of the island's small jungle and tore out a limb from the brush. He beat at the sand

and chased after the scorpion that had given him the wake-up call. Kyle was hungry and miserable enough not to laugh out loud. But he would hate to see something like this after he'd had a cup of coffee.

"Did it sting you?" he asked.

Win stopped and looked at Kyle. Win was bent at the shoulders, the limb dragging from his fingers. He was panting and his eyes were bloodshot. If ever anyone looked like the transition from ape to caveman, it was Win just then.

"You're damn right it stung me," he shouted.

"It's no worse than a hornet sting, Dad. It won't kill you," Kyle said. "Is your heart okay?"

"My heart's just goddamned fine."

Then Kyle realized for the first time that what he was seeing was some version of alcohol withdrawal.

A painful moan came from under the other rain jacket that still covered the lump between dunes that was Chaz. The jacket fell away as Chaz slowly sat up, and Kyle stumbled a step back. Chaz's face was swollen into a couple of dark purple and black bruises that contrasted with his blond hair—that and mosquito bites and a rash that swept up his arms and covered his neck.

Kyle did not have to ask. He walked up the beach a few steps until he located the sticks Chaz had cut to catch water with his rain jacket during the rain. The sticks had the dark blotches of resin along their bark. Poisonwood.

Kyle turned away from the two unhappy campers and went to get his fly rod and catch breakfast.

The water felt good as he waded in. It was the best

thing he could have done for the mosquito bites, rather than sit and be miserable on the sandy beach. But providence was kind to the fish that morning. He cast until he could barely raise the rod, but he had only a few missed hooksets on short strikes. He waded back to the shore. The three of them had to settle for gnawing at pieces of coconut washed down with sips of their precious water.

The tide had started to come in, but the boat had been pushed to the top of the high tide mark by the storm. Kyle sat looking at the boat. His father was looking up at the clearest blue sky they had experienced so far on the trip.

"What I can't figure is why no one is looking for us," he said. "We should have heard a 'copter or plane by now."

Kyle thought of several answers, but left all of them alone.

"What the hell can Margo be up to?" Win added.

Chaz was miserable enough to be silent. The rash had swept to other parts of him, and he sat stiff and immobile. One eye was swollen almost shut. The other squinted from his slow moving head with enough venom to discourage even the most polite query about how he felt. His breathing sounded harsh, as if drawing each breath was a struggle. Kyle, for the first time, felt sorry for Chaz and worried about him. He hoped the breathing problem had nothing to do with the beating he had given his brother. Maybe his father was right. Kyle had too much compassion to run the business the way Win hoped it would be run. But they had better get his heir back to civilization soon if he wasn't going to choke himself. Chaz's labored breathing was the only sound as they ate.

Kyle gave a start. His eyes opened wider as he stared at the boat.

"What is it?" Win snapped at him.

"I might be able to fix it," he said.

"The boat?"

"Of course."

"Well, dammit. Do it."

Kyle rose and went over to a stand of tall sea oats that grew along the edge of the sea grape bushes. He picked several of the longest and stiffest of them.

"We'll need to get some rollers and get the boat out into the water and anchor it," he said.

"Are you that sure of yourself?"

Kyle was, and he was ticked at himself for not thinking of it sooner. The boat's siren should have made him think of it, but the chaos of the trip so far, and the business with his father's inheritance had clouded his thoughts. Now he saw it the way he should have all along.

His confidence was so high that he stowed his fly rod and duffle bag on the boat before they started.

The sun was beating down on them with all it had by the time the high tide was all the way up the beach. They had been able to wrestle the boat so that its bow pointed toward the water. As the waves lapped higher they eased the boat onto rows of small sticks and twigs until they were able to push it to the water's edge. Then the boat slowly eased in itself as it slid down the beach, each wave lifting it and pulling it out a bit further as they shoved in timing to the waves.

At last it rocked free from the beach and Kyle and Chaz were able to pull it out into waist deep water and anchor it. Win stood on the shore, his hands on his hips, and his very red face watching them.

Kyle and Chaz climbed up into the boat. Kyle lowered the trim of the motor until just the tip of the motor's propeller was in the water. The electric motor sounded fine, which encouraged him.

"Why don't we try the motor?" Chaz said.

"Don't waste the electric," Kyle said. "Let me clear the intake first. That's the problem. The impeller can't haul water into the motor to cool the engine and the motor has an automatic shut off."

He climbed down the ladder and eased one of the sea oat stems up through one of the intake slots on either side of the motor's column. When they had rested on the sand and mud while being stranded high and dry by the tide they must have sucked in some mud. Why hadn't he thought of that before? Chaz's struggle to breathe had been what made him think of it at all.

Now that he knew they would be off the island soon, he enjoyed it more than before. He looked across at the tops of the swaying palms, at the very green of the mass of gumbo-limbo trees. The saltwater was cool and refreshing as he hung from the ladder with an arm around the motor's post. Below he could see the small gobi he had spotted earlier dart back and forth around a spiny urchin on the sand.

He cleared out both sides of the intake, then scrambled back up the ladder. He nudged Chaz away from the console and lowered the trim until the prop was underwater, then gave the key a twist. The motor coughed and started. He let it warm. On the shore he saw Win rushing into the water, leaving everything on the shore.

Chaz had settled up in the bow, bent over and scratching at his rash. He looked as defeated and miserable as Kyle could hope for, but it did not make him happy. He just wanted to get off the island too.

Win clambered up the ladder and rushed dripping to the console. "Pull anchor," he snapped.

Kyle lifted the diving ladder first and secured it, then went up to the anchor and hauled it up. Chaz made no effort to help.

Win put the boat in gear and headed it out toward the cut and the open ocean.

Kyle eased up and stood beside him at the console as the boat slipped through the gap in the reef.

Win's hand started to pull the throttle all the way open and Kyle had to grab at the chrome railing around the console. His father's head turned toward him, and he glared. The words were tugged away by the wind, but Kyle was pretty sure his father had shouted, "Why the hell didn't you think of that sooner?"

BETTY SUE STUCK HER head inside the tasting room door. "Good news, everyone. The Castles have started on their way back here. Win and the boys made it back to the hotel."

The last visitors to the tasting room had just left, the door locked behind them. Boose was helping Esbeth clean off the counters while Pearl was adding up the day's sales.

"Any chance a getting them to take the long way back?" Boose said.

"We're just glad they're all alive and coming home," Pearl said.

Betty Sue ducked back out the door.

"Don't you have an opinion, Esbeth?"

Esbeth looked up from sponging the marble bar top. She was tired and a little cranky, but there was nothing new in that. "I try not to belabor the obvious—" she frowned "—or I'd have a tattoo on my butt that says 'Slippery When Wet.'"

"BUT YOU SAVED THEM, didn't you?" Cassie's face was almost pressed against Kyle's as she leaned across the arm rests of the first class seats. He had never thought before how very much she looked like his mother when she was mad. He tried to think back to when he met her, but it seemed she had just suddenly been there in college, already a part of his life.

He waved a hand low to hush her. "It wasn't quite like that."

Win and Margo sat in the seat ahead of them, and Kyle was glad he could not see their faces.

"But that old bastard is still going to give the estate over to Chaz, isn't he?" she whispered in a fierce rasp, her mouth pressed close to Kyle's ear.

"We'll see," Kyle whispered back. He tried to end the heated conversation. The flight attendant went by, but moved quicker when she saw Cassie's expression. The attendant had been making steady visits to the seat in front to keep their glasses full. Neither Win nor Margo seemed disposed to make the trip home sober. The silence that came from their seats was only interrupted by the click of their glasses being refilled several times. They must have thrashed out their differences in their hotel room the night before.

Chaz sat up a couple of rows across the aisle, his face wrapped in white like some mummy. Bea and the kids filled most of the rest of the first class compartment. Maggie and her new husband had stayed on in Belize for a few days, and the expression on Maggie's face had been one of relief as she saw the others off onto their plane.

"But you saved their lives, didn't you?" Cassie repeated. "Hold that up to them."

"That's not the way it works."

"It is if you want to hang onto what you had, what was yours by right anyway. Do you want to lose everything you had?"

"Does that include you?"

"You can bet your miserable spineless ass it does," she said.

"Let's talk about this when we're calmer." He knew she meant it, and he tried to care more. But he was too tired, or emotionally drained, to get there.

"I'm never going to be calmer about this."

"Wait until we're home."

"I'll be packing when we're home," she said. Her head was turned away toward the window, but he heard her mutter, "And I want my maiden name. I never liked being called Cassie Castle anyway."

"Ssshh."

"Don't you shush me, Kyle Castle. I don't care if your folks do hear. That old buzzard's doing you wrong, and me. He's going to bring you all down, and I don't want to be there when it happens."

Kyle looked away, trying to end the conversation. He

was thinking of a poem he had read somewhere long ago at college, a line of which went: "The streets are filled with Cassandras."

"I'LL HAVE ANOTHER glass of this swill you call wine," Win said.

The flight attendant bent closer. She was a tall and slender woman who wore her blond hair up in a bun. She spoke softly enough for just him to hear. "I believe you've had enough, sir."

He had barely touched the food on his plate, a portion of chateaubriand with a béarnaise sauce, surrounded by baby carrots and half a red potato. Margo was just finishing hers. She looked up and smiled at the flight attendant. "He's always this cross," she said. "The wine will calm him." To that she added her look of "Don't make us buy this airline just to fire you."

The attendant stood upright and went to the galley to get the bottle.

Margo leaned closer to Win. "Are you deliberately trying to embarrass me?"

"You don't need me for that," he said.

The attendant was back and filled his glass without making eye contact with either of them.

When she had gone back up the aisle, Margo said, "This sort of thing never happened in the Bremman family."

Win said nothing. He knew that mention of her maiden name always led to a listing of reasons why she should never have married him, how she'd had better opportunities, ones to which he had blinded her with whatever mystical power he had back in those days. She had probably been stirred to think of maiden names after hearing Cassie's comment to Kyle. It did not look good for the boy's marriage, but then, if he had known she was going to be barren, maybe he shouldn't have married her. Keeping the Castle name going was all that mattered to Win, all he had left. It was what drove him.

After a few minutes, Margo leaned close until she could whisper directly into Win's ear. "If you ruin poor Kyle's life over this, I'll never forgive you."

Win spoke more softly, but made no attempt to whisper. "I realize he's your favorite. But he doesn't have what it takes."

She leaned close again. "A mother doesn't have favorites." Her whisper had an edge to it. "What I'm fond of in Kyle is that he's most like you. I know you lean toward Chaz, always have. Is it because he's like me?"

Win turned to her, his head rocking back an inch as he did. He frowned, but did not have a ready answer.

"I just hope everything has a chance to get back to normal once we get back to Texas," Margo said.

"Normal?" Win looked at her.

FIVE

THE DARKER GRAPES were on all the vines nearest the house and other buildings. Esbeth stood in the tilled row beside a Merlot vine covered with bunches of purple grapes hanging in rows beneath the canes and tendrils that lifted onto the trellised lyre system. The sun beat down on her face and the wind tugged at her gray-white hair. A drop of sweat was forming on her nose, and she rubbed at it.

"I'd bend down there," Esbeth told the group of people who crowded close around her, "but you'd have to bury me on the spot, because I'd never be able to get back up."

Someone in the crowd tittered—a person near Esbeth's age, who understood better than the others.

"What I want you to notice is that lump in the vine's stem that's about six inches off the ground. That's where the plant was grafted when it was just a pup. We graft all the plants here on the grounds. That has a Texas wild mustang-based hybrid root combined with the more delicate upper Merlot plant. If it weren't for this kind of grafting of a tougher native root, wine grapes wouldn't do as well as they do in Texas vineyards."

Esbeth looked around at the faces gazing at the vine's base. "We owe everything to a fellow named T. V. Munson who settled up in Dennison, Texas. That's north of Dallas. He was a horticulturist, interested in classifying American grapes, who found strains of them that were resistant to phylloxera, root rot. In 1880, a phylloxera plague was sweeping through France, wiping out some of the most famous vineyards in the world. They finally got in touch with Munson, and he sent over bundles of his resistant rootstocks. He saved the crop, and was awarded their *Chevalier du Merite Agricole,* and, in 1888, he was inducted into their Legion of Honor. That's something to remember the next time you get any snooty down-the-nose treatment at some French restaurant."

Esbeth could not think of an occasion when she would be in such a restaurant herself, unless they served something like cornbread croissants and chicken-fried *pâté de foie gras,* which she doubted. But she could see the Texans in the crowd getting all puffy-chested about the idea. She waved the group to follow and headed back over toward the buildings. Win Castle had been one of the first in Texas to graft and plant the *Vitis vinifera* varieties with the resistant rootstocks, but she wondered if he remembered, or was as comfortable with the idea of humble roots being attached to his aristocratic plants.

She was more aware than she should have been that her feet hurt and she was tired as she led her crowd of fifteen people out of the warm breeze outside into the cool air of the fermentation room. Huge stainless steel tanks, each capable of holding 2,500 to 5,000 gallons and surrounded by various kinds of refrigeration coils, lined both walls.

"This is more like it," one of the men said. The temperature inside the room was around 50 degrees. It was over 100 degrees outside.

Esbeth agreed, though she held the door open until the last couple pushed a stroller through the door. Then she moved out into the cool of the room and stood in the front of the group to wave at the big tanks. "This is state of the art wine-making, whether you're in the Napa Valley or France. In Texas we have most of the fermentation tanks inside, because of the climate. The goal of a small winery like this is to get the grapes hand-picked off the vines, through the auger hopper, crusher-stemmer, and grape press we just saw into one of these tanks, a controlled environment where the serious fermentation can begin."

She saw one of the men at the back holding up a tentative hand. "You have a question?" she asked.

"Yeah. What's that guy up there doing?"

Esbeth turned and looked up. At the top of one of the fermentation tanks, a pair of boots at the bottom of a pair of jeans stuck out. They were not moving.

In the month since Win and the boys had returned, there had been enough changes around the winery that Esbeth couldn't tell if the legs belonged to Bill Markley, Win, or Chaz, the new assistant winemaster.

She turned back to the crowd. "The winemaster and assistant winemaster are constantly checking the progress of the wine during fermentation," she said, fighting not to let the furrows on her forehead deepen.

"Why isn't he moving?"

"I don't know that much about what they do up there,"

Esbeth admitted, "but it sometimes takes a while. Now, let's move right along to the barrel room where we get to see what happens to the red wines and the Chardonnay."

She herded the group through the next set of doors, one or two of them glancing up to the top of the tank where the feet had still not moved.

Esbeth had skipped the part about residual sugar levels in the wines and the different lengths of time and temperatures they are kept in the tanks, and all about how the longer they are in the tanks, the drier they become. But she was distracted by the bottoms of those boots. All of the men wore the same kind of Red Wing work boots in a Wellington-style, but the soles and heels of these had looked new.

"Just crowd into the barrel room there," she said, "and I'll be right behind you."

She shot around the corner and through the doors of the lab. Boose had his arms around a large bag of some kind of chemical while Bill sat on a stool in front of a row of partially filled wine glasses.

They both looked up when she barged in.

"Up on top of one of the fermentation tanks," she panted. "Someone's up there, and he's not moving."

"Oh, shit." Boose dropped the bag and ran out the door.

"Who?" Bill said. He got up more slowly and started out.

"Chaz, I think," Esbeth said.

Bill went to the fermentation room and closed the doors, while Esbeth caught up with her crowd.

"The reason we use oak—" she was having trouble getting her breath back "—is because it's strong, it can breathe, and it has a flavor to impart to the wine."

There was shouting in the next room and a few heads turned that way.

"But enough of this," Esbeth said. "Let's rush on to the next room where we'll see the bottling apparatus."

"Hey, wait a minute," one man said. "How many bottles does one of these hold?"

"More than any of us could drink at a sitting," she said. "Now, come on."

The man stood his ground.

"There's about sixty gallons in each," Esbeth said, "and the wine bottles go about five to the gallon. I'll let you do the math." That got the man moving.

"How long are they in here for?" a lady asked.

"Eighteen months for the red wine, about twelve weeks for the Chardonnay. Step lively now."

The crowd acted restless, uncertain. The pace was sure picking up on their leisurely tour.

Half the crowd was out the door when a man asked, "How come some of them have those white plastic-looking corks in the bungs, and others just a paper cup?"

"The paper cup ones also don't have a label. They're empty. They put sulphur dioxide gas in the barrels when they're empty to kill anything that might harm the next wine the barrel holds. Now, let's move. We want to look at the bottler."

"Is it going to get away?" the man kidded.

"It just might," Esbeth said.

She got everyone moving down the hall and away from

the fermentation room. But she glanced back at the doors that were still closed. Something was certainly not right back there.

SHERIFF ELDON WATKINS made it out to the winery in under twenty minutes, and the first thing he did was seal off the fermentation room with yellow "police line" tape.

Eldon had a hard, cowboy look about him, even though the hair that showed beneath his Smokey the Bear hat was gray, almost white.

Boose stood beside him, both of them leaning on the big stainless steel side of the auger hopper as they waited for the meat wagon, as Eldon called it.

"You think it was an accident?" Eldon asked Boose. Eldon was an inch or two shorter than Boose, and was round compared to Boose's lean hardness. But few people would have missed whatever showed in the sheriff's face after thirty years of riding the ups and downs of this county. He and Boose, like most of the folks in the small community, went back a long ways, hunting together and occasionally mixing in other social settings.

"All I can tell you is that it's a wonder you never came out here and found me like that," Boose said. "When you're up on top of one of those, banging away with a pole to break up a cap, you can damn near fall in half the time. I've come as close to killing myself that way as any other out here. I was trying to punch the cap open once and the pole broke. I fell halfway in, but I held my breath and was able to grab the edge and pull myself back up in time. Don't look like Chaz managed that."

"The cap's the lid?"

"No. It's the mass of grape skins that float to the top when you're fermenting red wine. They take a set, half as hard as cement, and you've got to break them up."

"Why's it dangerous to fall in? I'd've thought you'd like that, Boose."

"Hell, it'll kill you quicker than John Wesley Harding. That's almost solid CO_2 gas in the top of one of those tanks."

"I always thought the most dangerous thing could happen to anyone at a winery is to drink themself to death," Eldon said.

"Hell's fire. We got chemicals out here'd make your hair stand on end like some spooked porcupine."

"But was it an accident?" Eldon repeated.

"Looks like it to me."

"He had the tank open and just fell in?"

"I shoulda been up there helping him. I been supposed to follow him around and make sure he don't screw up. But I thought he'd already got ahead of me and had the cap open. Least, he told me earlier he had."

"How do you account for him being up there, then?"

"I don't, and I don't have to. All I know is that young Chaz is dead," Boose said. "You're the one's gonna get a hot-foot from Win and Margo from here on out. I guess that's something you gotta find out. An accident's possible, I know that. But I also know Chaz wasn't gonna get any Valentines from most the folks who work out here, myself included. He was a worthless little prick who was gonna be running this whole place one day."

"You think that's some kind of motive?"

"I ain't paid to think, Eldon. That's more up your line than mine."

ESBETH STOOD LEANING against the counter. Bill and Betty Sue Markley were beside her. Pearl was behind the counter at the cash register. They had put up the "Closed" sign and locked the front gate early, but Pearl still had to count the money at the close of the business day, even if it came three hours early. Boose entered from the back door.

Clive Abramson came in from the door nearest the house, looking distracted. Then Win, Margo, and Kyle all came into the room at the same time as the sheriff. Win was looking off at nothing, seemed to be having trouble focusing. Margo looked distraught. Every hair on her blond head was still in perfect place, but her eyes were puffy and red. Kyle stood on one side of her, Win on the other.

The sheriff stepped out into the middle of the room. "While the coroner's in there having a look at Chaz, I want you all to know I'm gonna look close into this. But my initial reaction's that the whole thing was an accident."

An angry puff of air was the only noise in the room, and heads turned to glance at Esbeth. She wore a bright pink Camelot Hills T-shirt, jeans, and sneakers, none of which disguised her age.

"You disagree, Miss…"

"Esbeth Walters," she said.

"Oh," he said. "I guess I've read about you." He fought to show no expression, but a faint sour lemon look showed through. "You helped out Sheriff Danvers that time, didn't you." It was a statement, not a question. "I hope you're not gonna make trouble here. This should be a fairly straight-forward and simple investigation."

He caught something in Esbeth's look. "Do you have any hard evidence I don't?"

"I suspect you'll have some after the autopsy," she said.

"There won't be an autopsy if I can help it," Win said.

Kyle said nothing. Though he was sales manager now, he had also retained his title of public relations manager for the winery. He had not said much to any of them since Cassie had packed up and left as soon as the family arrived back in Texas from Belize. His mouth opened and then closed, but he just looked at his father.

"Don't be an ass," Margo said to Win. "Of course we want an autopsy."

"Oh, there'll be one," the sheriff said, "whether either of you want it or not."

"Eldon, do I need to remind you…"

"Win, whatever you were gonna say, do yourself a favor and don't say it," Eldon said. He was glancing around at the faces of the others in the room.

Esbeth watched two EMS workers push a body bag on a portable gurney swiftly past the windows of the tasting room.

"I'm gonna have my deputy, Chunk Philips, you all know him, come out and hang around until we get a result from the coroner," the sheriff said. He caught a look from Win. "I don't expect nothin', and when they let me know that, you'll all be free to go about your regular business."

"You'll hear from…"

"Don't even finish that, Win." Eldon spun toward the

winemaster and glared. "I'm giving you all every break here, so don't flap your wings and crow when you don't have to."

He dismissed them, and all of the Castles went out of the room and headed toward the house before Esbeth could say anything.

Sheriff Watkins glanced at Pearl, Boose, Clive Abramson, Bill and Betty Sue Markley, then Esbeth. "I'm sorry as hell about this, but I gotta ask that you wait here on the grounds till I hear back from the coroner."

"What, and sleep here on the floor?" Esbeth said.

Eldon looked at her, and his eyes narrowed a quarter inch. "If you're wrong and this is just an accident, you got no problem. I'll be sending you home 'fore it's dark. But if you think something's up, you should let me know now. You been noticing any tension around here?"

Esbeth gave him a tired, stubborn, and irritated squint back and said, "Have you noticed the weather being a tad warm?"

BOOSE AND PEARL kept Esbeth company in the tasting room. Bill and Betty Sue Markley were there too, but they hovered down at the far end of the counter talking to each other. Only a low mutter of their conversation got as far as Esbeth. Clive Abramson sat off by himself on a wooden bench in the corner. He had already been through the newspaper he held a time or two by now and had only spoken once to beef at Boose for having already filled in the crossword puzzle.

The light was beginning to fade outside and no mention

had been made by anyone of plans for supper or where they would sleep if Eldon Watkins insisted they stay the night.

Esbeth's stomach gave her a twinge, but she stayed away from the pretzels they offered so visitors could sample the Chenin Blanc mustard. Boose had dug out a ratty and dog-eared deck of cards, and he and Pearl were playing some kind of double solitaire across the top of the marble counter. Neither ever spoke much when around each other, Esbeth had noticed. For the moment that fit the mood.

She looked down at the pink T-shirt she still wore. "If I'd a choice, this wouldn't be the togs I'd be stuck in for more than a few hours," she said.

"Humpf." Boose looked at her, then back at the cards in front of him.

"I know you two live close to here," Esbeth finally said, "but I don't fancy a long drive in the dark to get home. Deer shoot into the road from all sides, and if it isn't them, there are all manner of other kinds of biological speed bumps out there."

"You're the one acting like it was no accident," Boose said.

"It wasn't," Esbeth said. "That's the shame of it."

"What makes you so sure?" Pearl asked.

Esbeth glanced at her, but there was too much innocence in the girl's eyes to even answer.

Bill and Betty Sue looked up from their intense chat, but neither spoke. Clive kept his head in his newspaper.

"I 'spect the Castles are at the dinner table just now," Boose said.

"We could order a pizza," Pearl said, "except no one delivers to way out here."

"And if we had ham, we could have ham and eggs, if we had eggs," Esbeth grumped.

"You want some dinner, just call over and ask the dragon lady if you can have the bones when they're done eating." Boose's tone had an edge to it.

"Boose," Pearl said.

"If she says, 'Let them eat cake' you can just…"

"Boose," Pearl almost shouted.

The door to the tasting room opened and Margo stuck her head inside. "I hope I'm not interrupting," she said. "Esbeth, can I talk to you?"

Esbeth shrugged and looked at Boose and Pearl. Betty Sue and Bill looked surprised that they had not been the ones asked to chat. Clive's paper rustled.

"I guess I've got an opening in my dance card," Esbeth said. She walked to the door and went out to join Margo, who stood out on the Spanish tiles beneath one of the crepe myrtle plants. Her interior designer background showed, since she had selected one with blooms a color that complemented her outfit.

"Sorry to tear you away, Esbeth." She took off at a walk and Esbeth took quick steps until she was in stride beside her. They walked out onto the crunch of gravel and followed the drive around where it skirted the Merlot plants, the big purple bunches of grapes hanging beneath the swaying green leaves of the arbors.

Margo kept her head slightly lowered, like a general thinking over troop maneuvers. Esbeth could not tell if Margo was still in shock or if she was at a later stage of mourning. There was evidence on Margo's face that she had been crying earlier, which only Esbeth's experience could spot. It was not an emotion Margo was comfortable sharing, and she had made her face over, but Esbeth knew what to look for. Margo was frowning to herself, but she finally looked over at Esbeth.

"You've had experience in this sort of thing," she said.

Esbeth nodded slowly, but Margo hardly noticed.

"I want to know what to expect next."

"Didn't the sheriff explain that?"

"I heard what he said to Win. I want your take on this."

"What do you mean?"

"What do you think will happen next?"

"If the coroner confirms it was an accident, we all go home and you folks are left to deal with your grief. I'm very sorry for you."

"I don't mean that." There was more steel in Margo's voice than Esbeth expected. "I mean if it goes the other way."

"Do you mean murder?"

Margo stopped and turned to look down into Esbeth's face. "I do."

Esbeth could look down the lane to the locked gate at the small road that passed the vineyard and see the sheriff's department patrol car where Chunk Philips leaned against a fender.

"Well," Esbeth said, "we'll all have a longer day of it, then. We'll be questioned, statements will be taken. Someone will have to come out from Austin, a Ranger, I expect. Then there'll be forensic crews, and…"

"And what?"

"Media, I suppose."

"Damn."

"There's no help for that. The Castles are a prominent family."

They had paused beside Margo's new white Mercedes, the one she had bought a month ago, in the same week Win had made Betty Sue lower everyone's wages and hours because the last few batches of wine hadn't sold as well as they should have.

"If it comes to that, Esbeth, can I count on you?" Margo glanced over at Esbeth.

"For what?" Esbeth looked up at the face that seemed to be having a wrestling match to show no emotion. She hoped she was not going to be asked to lie, because she already knew her own answer to that.

"You've got a bit of a reputation as a detective. Could you poke around, see what you could find out?"

"Don't you think we'd better wait to see what Sheriff Watkins comes up with?"

"I have a fear," Margo said, "that comes from deep in my bones." She turned abruptly without explaining and began to walk again.

Esbeth had to take quick small steps to catch up to her.

"Who do you think they will suspect?" Margo asked.

"We're getting ahead of ourselves here," Esbeth said.

"Who?" Margo would not leave it alone.

"Well, I imagine the business about the boys competing will come up."

Margo's feet made the gravel whirl as she stopped and spun. "What do you know about that?"

"I imagine most the people in this part of the county

know about that," Esbeth said. "There's Cassie leaving Kyle, as well as Clive Abramson and Bill Markley both being demoted. This is a tiny little piece of a small county. People talk."

"Little people always talk too much, don't they?"

"I don't know about that," Esbeth said. "I've been in big cities too and folks there jaw about as much."

"I think it's pathetic," Margo said, making no effort to mask the hostility in her tone.

The sun was close to the horizon, and the sky was shifting to bands of purple across a pink background. Rising from far down the road, Esbeth could see a long lifting swirl of dust.

One minute Esbeth was looking away from Margo's haughty profile, then the next moment she felt hands grabbing her by the shoulders of her T-shirt, pulling her close. Esbeth realized her face was an inch from Margo's, and the eyes that looked down at her were like open doors to a furnace. "If they ever catch whoever did this to my Chaz." Flecks of angry spit landed on Esbeth's cheek.

Margo's face suddenly shifted, showed more doubt, but no regret. She let go and took a half step back. Esbeth's head reeled, and she felt a sudden chill, having been face-to-face with the woman's inner dragon.

"Maybe you're right," Margo said, her tone deflating like a balloon out of air. "It could just be an accident. But my poor dead Chaz…" Her head bent and she grabbed Esbeth by the shoulders and clutched her, more gently this time, pressing her face to Esbeth's round shoulder. Margo began to sob as if her heart had been torn out.

Esbeth watched the road, saw the other sheriff's cruiser followed by two other cars, one of them an unmarked car with a high police antenna and search lights. The caravan slid up to the front gate, then accelerated as they went to the delivery entrance and began to come up that lane, raising red clouds of dust beside the rows of Chardonnay.

Esbeth didn't say anything to Margo, even if she had been able to, but she knew for certain now that it had been no accident.

TILLIS MACRORY shoved a cassette into his car's tape player and looked back up at the green rolling slopes of Texas Hill Country as he drove to look into yet another murder. The car speakers pounded out an old Bob Dylan cut of, "If I Had It To Do All Over Again, I'd Do It All Over You." It was the second anniversary of Tillis's divorce. Funny, for eleven years he had not been able to remember their anniversary, but he remembered their divorce. Claire always said he was married to the Texas Rangers anyway. Maybe she was right. Well, hell, of course she was. She had been right about a lot of things.

In this part of Texas it was possible to start noticing the same kind of fence running along the road for several miles. These were spreads—big ones, some with oil as well as cattle. Others diversifying to keep up with the times—putting up dude ranches, bed and breakfast getaways, or selling out all the way and developing into clusters of suburban-like homes. But there was no water way out here, except the lakes and deep wells, and that kept some of the building down. Most of the hills were still speckled with green dots of mesquite, sage, scrub cedar, and occasional live oaks, like the thick-trunked hangman's tree he was passing.

Up ahead he could see, in the fading light of late afternoon, cream and sandy buildings rise up out of rows of grape vines, like some small castle highlighted with the hues of the sunset. Behind the buildings he could see the lake, big and stretching out for miles. Lake Fredonia was a deep lake, noted for its striped bass. They were stocked by the wildlife commission, and were no more able to reproduce than the steers that fed in all the fields he had passed getting here.

A sheriff's car and the car with the forensics crew were waiting along the side of the road for him. He slowed and waved. The deputy pulled out and led the way down the road and to a back service entrance that led in red dirt and gravel along the grape vines back to the buildings. The three cars pulled up and gave the dust a moment to settle.

Macrory got out of the car, put on his white hat, and stretched. He talked with the forensics crew, and they went on toward the fermentation room. The deputy waited on Macrory, then led the way to the house. They crossed the courtyard and went in. He spotted Sheriff Eldon Watkins standing and looking uncomfortable; the woman and a younger man sat on a couch while the older man paced.

"Eldon," Macrory said.

The sheriff introduced him to the family members: Win, Margo, and Kyle Castle. Macrory took what early impressions he could. The woman and the boy had been crying. The father still looked as outraged as he would be if the laws of gravity were suspended. Things like this apparently didn't happen to people named Castle.

"I'm sorry about all this," Macrory addressed the Castles, "and I'm going to cut right to it here. I've talked with the coroner and we've brought in our own M.E., um, Medical Examiner. There was some CO_2 in Charles's body, but there was sulphur dioxide first. Can you tell me anything about either chemical?"

Since shaking hands with the Ranger, Win had settled onto the arm of the couch near Margo. He stood to speak. "We use sulphur dioxide in the oak barrels after they've had wine in them. It kills anything likely to harm the aging of the next wine we put in them. But Chaz was up on top of one of the fermentation tanks. That's where CO_2's a big risk. Are you sure that's not what killed him? He might have picked up some secondary exposure to the sulphur dioxide elsewhere. We all try to be careful around here, but there is a risk."

"No. It was SO_2. I wouldn't be here if we weren't absolutely positive that sulphur dioxide was the cause of death. You're aware of the 9850 Sulphur Dioxide Analyzer that uses UV fluorescence to measure concentrations of sulphur dioxide?"

"No." It was the first demure word Macrory had heard from Win. Macrory had not heard of the machine himself until a few minutes ago in a conversation with the M.E. There'd been a death at one of the other of Texas' thirty or so vineyards, an accident as that one turned out, where the M.E. had to acquire the machine. He'd brought it along as soon as he heard where he was headed this time. Macrory wasn't even sure if that was the gadget the M.E. had used to come to his conclusion. But he was glad for the information if it took some of the chip off Win Castle's shoulder.

Macrory noticed something else. When Win spoke, his eyes moved all around the room, but he never let his eyes connect with Kyle's. There might be something to that.

"I'll want to talk with you each individually," Macrory said. "Let me ask you three as the family first, is there any reason any of you can think of why anyone might want to kill Charles?" He concentrated on watching their faces, especially Kyle's. But the boy looked truly sad. The mother, Margo, put her face in her hands and began to sob. Win glared at her, as if she were revealing a weakness. When Macrory looked up from her, it was Win who spoke.

"Don't be ridiculous. Chaz was a strong-willed young boy. But no one hated him. You'll see when you talk to the others. You'll find in the end that this was almost certainly an accident of one kind or another. But I'm sure you'll pester us all to distraction," he snapped.

"I will sure try to," Macrory promised, not smiling.

When they left the house, and were ushering the Castles over to the tasting room for Macrory to meet the others, Sheriff Watkins held back and leaned closer to Macrory to say, "You get a lot of hill-billy cowboys out this way who think they're aristocracy. But don't get me wrong. Most of the people out here are swell—folksy and as friendly as bed bugs. But the ones you gotta watch out for are those with a couple of coins to rub together, especially ones they didn't earn themselves."

They were all back in the tasting room. Esbeth's insides were churning from having no supper and knowing what was to come.

One of the men from the forensics crew was helping set up folding chairs. Hot as it was outside, he was wearing a lightweight black jacket that said in big letters across the back: CRIME SCENE. Esbeth let herself plop into one of the chairs. She sighed and waited on the inevitable.

All the Castles were present except Bea, who lived four miles down the road and had been given a sedative while her regular sitter came to watch the kids. Clive Abramson was still in the room, as was Boose, Pearl, and Bill and Betty Sue Markley.

Maggie and Howie were still in Belize on their honeymoon. That was going to be a phone call Esbeth figured Margo would not enjoy making.

Win's face was flushed an almost solid red, and Esbeth would not have been surprised if he keeled over at any moment. Margo sat stern and unsmiling in her chair, as far from tears now as any mother could ever be under the circumstances. Kyle looked restless and a bit nervous. But he sat and stared toward the lawmen at the end of the room.

Esbeth focused on the man standing beside Sheriff Eldon Watkins who wore a light blue serge jacket over khaki trousers and boots. She caught the edge of the Mexican silver glitter of the badge pinned above his left shirt pocket. He was gray at the temples beneath the edge of the white cowboy hat he wore indoors, but looked like someone who had lifted weights when he was younger.

Now his tired and wise eyes were running across the faces of the people in front of him in a way Esbeth knew far too well.

Eldon made sure they were all settled before he spoke. "I'd like to introduce you all to Tillis Macrory. He's with the Texas Rangers."

Margo made a gasping sound, even though Esbeth knew that Eldon or the Ranger would have taken the Castles aside and given her and Win a hint of what to expect.

"He'll be talking with you all one by one. As some of you folks already know, the coroner, on closer examination, has been able to determine that Charles Castle didn't die of CO_2 poisoning, as we first suspected."

The Texas Ranger, Tillis Macrory, eased up and put his hand on Eldon Watkin's shoulder. "Maybe I had better brief them, Eldon."

"Oh, yeah. Sure." Eldon took a step back and waited. He glanced over at Win.

"We haven't ruled out death by accident," Macrory said. "But we want to be very careful and run a thorough investigation at this point. Is that understood?"

He was looking at their faces, stopped when he came to Esbeth. She felt like a puddle slumped in her chair, but after a minute of his stare she sat up straighter.

"Some of you have had suspicions since the incident happened. I want you to keep your speculations to yourself until we talk in private. Understand?" His eyes were very intense, and locked with Esbeth's now.

He finally broke free and looked at the others. "Just one quick general question first. Which of you is Boose?"

Boose held up a hand and tilted his head a quarter inch to the right.

"I understand you're best suited to tell me this, what was Charles Castle supposed to be doing up on top of that fermentation tank?"

Win started to speak and Macrory held up the flat of his hand to him. He stared at Boose.

Boose glanced around the room, then looked back at the Ranger. "When you ferment white wine," he said, "you only use the juice. But with red wine you use the skins and everything. The skins float, and form a thick cap. After a while you need to open the top of the tank and use a pole to break up the cap. Then you can run a pump to circulate the juice so the skins get exposed to all the wine for maximum flavor. Later the skins'll be removed in the wine press."

"I could have told you that," Win said.

Macrory ignored him. He asked Boose, "And you thought Charles had already done this?"

"He told me he had. That's all I know."

"Any reason he might have gone back up there?"

"He might've wanted to take a look and make sure the cap had stayed broken up," Boose said.

Esbeth made a small noise in spite of herself.

The Ranger's head turned slowly to her. "What is it, Miss Walters?"

She shook her head.

"Go ahead. What do you think we'll find?"

Esbeth cleared her scratchy throat. She was tired, hungry, and more irritable than usual. But she fought to keep her voice polite. "It's what you won't find," she said.

"And that is?"

"Fingerprints on the ladder going up to the tanks."

Macrory glanced at the sheriff, then looked back at Esbeth. He started to say something, then stopped himself. "Let me take a slightly different slant on what I was going to ask. Do you think it's possible that someone carried him up there?"

"All I know," Esbeth said, "is that I doubt if I could've lifted him an inch off the ground. I'm not trying to make excuses for myself, just share one of the universal truths about this case. I should wait until you determine if it was an accident."

"We'll have to wait on the toxicology report from our forensics people for that," he said. "But in the meantime…"

One of the men in the black CRIME SCENE jackets opened the tasting room door and motioned to Macrory. He stopped and went over to lean closer, let the man whisper directly into his ear. When he stood upright, he turned and let his eyes play across the group again.

He walked back to where he had stood and turned to face them.

"We now know that there are almost no fingerprints on the ladder or the top of the fermentation tank, just those of the coroner." He turned to Boose. "Weren't you the first up there?"

"Yeah, but I've seen a lot of dead things, and he looked like one of them. That and his head was hanging in the top of the tank, which I knew would've killed him."

There was a sobbing gasp from Margo.

"Why weren't your prints there too?"

"Look, I pulled him offa there by his belt, got no pulse, then I left the rest to you guys. I own a TV like most of the rest of America. I wasn't gonna leave no fingerprints. But I didn't wipe none out. I just didn't leave none either. Hell, I wasn't thinking too different from the old coot, er, Miz Walters, there." He gave Esbeth a quick half grin that somehow looked more like the grimace of a small wild animal with one leg in a steel trap. "If you were from here you'd understand. I knew from the get-go I was at a crime scene. That's all she'n'I are saying." Boose's face settled into a grumpy but defensive frown.

"We'll talk later." Macrory shifted his focus to the others in the room. "Though I still need the report from our own M.E., I believe we can proceed with this new information in mind."

He turned to look at Esbeth. "Before we begin, are there any more universal truths you feel compelled to share?"

"I'm surprised that someone like you gets anything out of trying to mock an old raisin like me."

That rocked his head back an inch. He said, in a slightly chastened tone, "I only meant that someone of your venerable years and experience with this sort of thing might have picked up another universal truth or two."

"Well, I'll give you one for free," she said.

"What's that?"

"If you *have* got a murder on your hands…"

"Yeah?"

She hesitated and glanced around, then said, "It's a certain bone cold fact that the murderer is someone sitting in this room."

SIX

"SEND IN THE next one," Macrory said.

Chunk Philips, in his deputy sheriff uniform, stood at the door that led from the living room out onto the courtyard. He turned and stepped outside; in a few moments he was back with Boose trailing behind him.

The Texas Ranger sat at one end of a couch in the living room. He had taken off his white cowboy hat. A soft leather briefcase was open on the couch beside him and he held a notebook. A tape recorder sat on the coffee table. Macrory waved to the sofa on the other side of the coffee table. Boose frowned and drug himself around to the front of the couch and plopped into the middle with an exaggerated sigh.

The windows were all black onyx squares. It was night outside. The lights were on, showing the tapestries, paintings, antique chairs, the deer antler chandelier, and the other bric-a-brac that was crowded into the room.

Macrory looked up from his notepad at Boose. "You seem a bit irritated by all this."

"Oh, don't mind me. I'm always like this," he said. "When I'm in the hospital, folks send the nurses get-well cards."

"You're not related to Miss Walters, by any chance, are you?"

"Naw. She's just grumpy 'cause she's old and hasn't eaten. Don't get me wrong, though. I like the old coot."

"I can tell." Macrory reached over and pushed a button on the recorder. "I want to focus on the incident, if I might, Boose. Any problem with that?"

"No."

"Good. When we're done here we'll send all of you home, though we want you to stay near your homes until we get a finding from the lab. You're from near here anyhow, aren't you?"

"Yeah, right down the road."

"Born in this area?"

"Yeah. My mother was here at the time, and I thought it'd be a good idea to be close."

Macrory's head snapped up from his pad.

"I been out here longer than dirt," Boose said. He looked it too. A bit of the dirt was beneath his fingernails and along one cheek of his rough, unshaved face.

"Let's focus on the issue at hand here," Macrory said. He had been around people like Boose all his life, knew that some of them liked to hear themselves talk just for the joy of the accent rattling around, others liked to spin a yarn or speak in colorful ways. There was nothing alarming in that, as far as it went.

"If this turns out to be murder, will that surprise you?"

"No."

"Why's that?"

"Will you know what I mean if I describe Chaz as the afterbirth of a cluster fu—"

Macrory held up a hand and stopped Boose in midsentence. "Let's keep this as tame as we can, Boose. Okay? Color's all right. But stay on track, if you can. I take it you weren't over fond of the victim."

"Your task is gonna be finding someone who was," Boose said. "Besides his mother, I mean, and she probably had days."

"But, wasn't Win Castle in the process of changing his will to make Charles his principal heir?"

"I guess you talked to Win and Margo already, so you know about Win getting Kyle and Chaz to knock heads over that."

Macrory nodded slowly.

"But Chaz getting the estate didn't mean Win liked him. It meant he thought he was as ruthless a prick as himself, and Win can be one of the prickliest."

Macrory frowned and glanced at the recorder again.

Boose noticed, but did not seem to care. He said, "Let me ask you, is it just as illegal for someone rich to lie, steal, or kill as me?"

"Of course."

"Well, let's keep that in mind through all of this."

"You didn't necessarily like Charles, but you got along with him okay. Is that about right?"

"Yeah, he wasn't likable, but he was a tolerable little prick until someone knocked his phone off the hook."

"You said earlier that you were supposed to be keeping an eye on Charles while he learned the ropes. How did he come to be up in a dangerous area without you?"

"That area isn't dangerous most of the time. For the part that can be, knocking a cap of grape skins apart before we circulate the juice to get rich color and flavor, I'm usually around. But he specifically told me he'd already broke the cap loose. I was getting a bag of potassium metabisulphite over into the room we keep locked when all this happened."

"You have chemicals so dangerous that you keep them locked?"

"Hell, yes."

"What do you use the…the chemical you just named for?"

"Potassium metabisulphite. We add it when we process the grapes. It's to keep the juice from starting to ferment on its own. We use special yeasts for the fermentation."

"Sounds like there're a lot of chemicals out here. Who has access to them?"

"Just about everyone here has a key, even a couple of the field hands. About the only ones who don't are the sales and tasting room staff."

"What were you doing between the time you saw Charles last and until he was found?"

Boose's eyes narrowed, and he did not answer right away. Macrory leaned closer to the coffee table. "Well?"

"I was with Bill Markley in the lab. Why do you want to know?"

Macrory hesitated this time, then said, "Because I'm working through opportunity as well as motive at the moment, keeping in mind that we may yet find this was an accidental death."

"You might be climbing up a fool's hill there," Boose said. "But don't let me stop you if you know the way."

"I'm just saying we need to hear from the lab."

"And what'll they have to say about Chaz wiping away all fingerprints before having his accident?" Boose said.

"That *is* the nub of our problem at the moment," Macrory admitted.

ESBETH CAME INTO the room when Chunk Philips ushered her in, and she felt a mixture of apprehension and relief. Macrory looked up at her.

"I hope you don't plan on trying to be snappier than Boose," he said.

"Oh no," she said. "I appreciate your waiting to the very last, though, to talk to the one person who has to drive the farthest to get home."

Macrory took a deep breath. "Go ahead and sit down."

She did, looking around at the clutter of antiques, paintings, and other items that filled every available space in the room. She settled on the deer antler chandelier. "Do you think Margo studied her interior designing under Randolph Hearst?"

"I know about Xanadu," Macrory said. "We're going to make better time if we stick to what matters here."

"Sure." Esbeth shrugged. She glanced at the dark of the windows outside, then to the tall grandfather clock along one wall. If she could get through this, she might get headed home barely in time to swing through the last fast food place on the outside of civilization and grab a bacon cheeseburger with fries. Damn the diet. She had been fixating on the cheeseburger for hours, and maybe a malted milk too.

"Um, Miss Walters."

"Yeah." She focused on the Texas Ranger.

"Was something on your mind?"

"So, let's see," she said, leaning forward on the sofa. "I was with a group when I found Chaz, and before that Pearl and I had our hands full in the tasting room with a bus load of winos posing as a senior citizens' outing. That kind of rules out opportunity. As for motive, I didn't know Chaz well enough to have more than a mild dislike for him, not near enough for murder."

"I'm not thinking of you as a suspect, Miss Walters."

"Esbeth," she said, "unless you want to make me think you're one of my math students from back in my high school teaching days."

"Okay, Esbeth." Macrory grinned, tired as he must be.

Esbeth knew she was exhausted to the bone herself, but she would gladly drink a cup of coffee if one was offered, even if it kept her up until next week. She did not fancy playing dodge-em cars with the wildlife and other night traffic while half asleep.

"What did you think about the competition Win Castle had stirred up between the two boys?"

"I think you'd have more of a case about that if Kyle had been the one that was dead. Besides, they'd settled all that. It was a done deal, and Win was changing his will. Everyone here knows that."

"But he hadn't."

"He may anyway. A person who threatens others with changing his will a lot can't really be the poster boy of a functional family, do you think?"

"Listen, Esbeth," Macrory leaned closer, his expression open and sincere, "I know you're tired, and I don't blame you. But the truth is, I saved you for the last for a selfish reason."

"You're kind of young for me, aren't you?"

His head cocked a bit to the left. "Are you sure you're not some distant relative of Boose?"

She gave him her most irritable squint.

"Never mind," he said. "I saved you for the last because I want to ask for your help and cooperation."

"It's a bit late to sugar-coat the pill," she said.

"No, I mean it. I know Sheriff Watkins has his reservations…."

"Just like the Indians."

He chose not to hear her. He said, "…but I think you can be a help to me if we put our heads together a bit. I'm new here. You have experience and have been a fly on the wall for a while. That could be invaluable to me."

"What kind of help do you want?" she said, still not sure if she believed him.

"Let's start through the players," he said. "What do you think of Margo Castle?"

"The general opinion around these parts is Leona Helmsley, maybe Marie Antoinette. But she wouldn't have killed her own son."

"I understand you. And Win?"

"King Lear comes to mind," she said. "But he just picked Chaz as his heir. There's no way he'd have had anything to do with his death."

"That's not what I mean," Macrory said. "I just wanted

your take on him. There are people I can eliminate from my consideration. You and Pearl were together, for instance."

She nodded.

"And Boose?" he said.

"Boose likes to talk gruff, but he's halfway raised those boys, taught them everything they knew about hunting."

"How about Kyle? Of all of them, he has the most obvious motive."

"You're going to have to get more from the family about him. But from everything I've seen, he lacks the spine for that sort of thing. It was the whole issue with his father, I understand."

"A lot of people who don't have the sand to shoot someone will have it to poison them," Macrory said. He looked down at his notes.

Esbeth was thinking back to what Maggie had said about poison being the likely way to murder anyone at a vineyard.

She cocked her head at the Ranger, watched him flip through his notes. "Your job is the most important thing in the world to you, isn't it?"

His head lifted, the lines on his forehead deeper than they had been.

"What brought that on?" he asked.

"I just mean that you would understand an obsession about a career, wouldn't you?"

"I guess I would." He looked away, said in a lower voice, "I had a birthday go by not too long ago and I didn't even think about it until a couple of weeks later."

"Well, don't feel bad," Esbeth said. "A lot of people are that way. It doesn't mean you have to go to weekly meetings in some church basement, where you have to get up and tell everyone else how you're doing. It's just what you've chose, nothing more than that."

"You're sowing seeds about something all the time, aren't you?"

She gave an over-elaborate shrug.

He shook himself and got back on track. "What about Clive?"

Esbeth looked up. She had been consciously not leaning back onto the sofa, afraid she would get so comfortable she might never get up. She felt as tired as a sore tooth. Her head gave a snap and she had to concentrate.

"He's certainly one unhappy camper right now," she said. "His job was taken away and given to Kyle. He has to settle for handling Kyle's sales territory for a lower salary, if he wants to stay at all."

"Does that seem fair?"

"Of course not. But I doubt if fair ever entered the Castle reasoning."

Macrory was making notes on his pad. He looked up again. "I understand Bill Markley had something of a career setback as well."

"His assistant winemaster spot was given to Chaz. But I suppose now that Chaz is gone, Bill will be back where he was. I guess you could make a case for motive out of that."

Macrory lifted an eyebrow. "Betty Sue?"

Esbeth snorted before she realized and caught herself.

"Sorry," she said. "But you were kind of making a case earlier for someone maybe carrying Chaz up to the top of that tank. I think you might be onto the right track with the idea, at least pursuing variations of that possibility. But you've seen Betty Sue. I doubt if she could carry someone her own size up that ladder. Besides, she's got such a nice disposition most of the time. I'd hate to think it was her. She's one of the little people, like the rest of us."

"But with a husband who just had a salary and dignity cut," Macrory said.

"You can go out on that limb, if you like," Esbeth said. "But I'm too tired to stretch with you just now."

"Then why don't you go home? But stay around there in case I need to reach you."

"You don't have a worry there," she said. "There's a phone by my bed, and if I have the strength to lift an arm to answer it, you'll be able to reach me."

THE LIGHTS WERE ON in the tasting room when Esbeth left the living room of the house. She crossed the courtyard and skirted around the separate building, walked out to her car, and sagged into the driver's seat. She gave herself a couple of brisk pats on either cheek and said, "Okay, old girl. All you've got to do is get home somehow."

She started the car, turned on the lights, and went down the delivery drive. A sheriff's department patrol car was blocking the drive. Sheriff Watkins himself sat behind the wheel. When he saw who it was, he backed up enough to let Esbeth's car go past. Then he slid the patrol car back into place.

Esbeth realized why as soon as she started up the road. Three vans, all wearing satellite disks on top, were parked by the front gate along with several other cars. Flash bulbs went off and she was blinded for a second. When she looked up, someone had run in front of her car and was waving his arms. He had a microphone in one hand, a cord trailed behind him, and a man with a camera on his shoulder was running to catch up to him.

Esbeth rolled up her window and locked her car door on that side. She waited until the man with the mike came around to the driver's side window, then she accelerated. She recognized the fellow, but had no urge to see herself on television beside him.

His face had a startled look as he bounced off the side of her car. It was the same look she suspected buzzards have when they are shooed away by traffic from a road kill.

She imagined for a moment she heard someone calling out about the public wanting to know. But she concentrated on keeping her eyes open and staying on the road all the way to her home.

THE PHONE RANG and Esbeth's eyes snapped open. The trip home late at night had a distant dream-like quality. She had not stopped for food, even though a few of the fast food places were open that late. She looked around the room for a disoriented moment, saw it was her own bedroom.

"Whew." The phone rang again, and she reached for it.

"Esbeth, is that you?" It was Margo Castle's voice.

"What? What?" She was looking down at herself beneath the covers. Light was coming in around the edges of the drawn drapes. The clock beside the bed said it was almost nine o'clock. She could not recall when she had slept so late, but she was not even sure when she had gotten home, though she did have her pajamas on, at least.

"Yeah, it's me," she said at last.

"Oh, dear. Am I calling too early? I forgot all about your long drive home." Margo gave one of her fake chuckles.

She had forgotten about the help going without their suppers too, but Esbeth did not mention that, although her stomach was letting her know.

"What is it?" Esbeth said.

"That Texas Ranger is back," Margo said, "as well as those jackals from the press. I don't know what we'll do when it's time to open the front gates."

"I think the public would understand if you don't open, since there's been a death in the family."

"Oh, I guess we could do that, but I would hate to turn away customers."

Esbeth thought of several responses, but all were too candid to share.

"Do you think you could make it out here and help us?" Margo asked.

"Give tours and tastings?"

"No. With all that's going on? Something Ranger Macrory didn't tell the rest of you, or give out to the media, was what exactly it was that killed Chaz."

"Then he wasn't poisoned?"

"He was poisoned, all right. But it wasn't from the CO_2, it was from exposure to sulphur dioxide gas, the kind they use to clean the barrels between uses."

"Then how did he end up on top of a fermentation tank?"

"That seems to be what's puzzling Mr. Macrory. It's way beyond anything Eldon Watkins could handle now. Can you come out?"

"And get in the way?"

"No. To help. Have you seen the papers? The things they're saying about us are just awful. We need this solved as soon as possible. And Mr. Macrory said some glowing things about you, said you're a lot sharper than you seem."

"Thanks, I think."

"Oh, you know what I mean. I'm so rattled by all this. I would feel so much better knowing you're here. Every little bit will help. Maggie's flying home. She and Howie are cutting their honeymoon short. But they'll be no help with all this. She asked about you too."

"Let me get dressed and something to eat," Esbeth said, "and I'll see what I can do."

"Oh, dear. You poor things must have been starved last night."

There was never any way to tell how genuine Margo's concern was, but it seemed to Esbeth that the woman was more concerned with not having done the socially correct thing than with the empty stomachs of the help.

"I'll make up for it this morning. I'll probably need some exercise after what I plan to eat," Esbeth said.

She hung up the phone and got up. Before she started making breakfast, she brought in the paper. The murder at the Castle vineyard had made the front page. But Esbeth put the paper on the table and made a small stack of buttered toast, six slices of bacon, three fried eggs, and a pot of coffee before she let herself sit down at the table and read what the public needed to know.

The lead story shared about as much as Esbeth knew. But she almost dropped that section of the paper into a half-eaten plate of eggs when she got to the sidebar story. She set the paper aside, finished eating, then refilled her coffee cup and pulled the paper closer. No wonder Margo had her expensive silk underwear wrapped into a knot.

After mentioning how the vineyard had progressed through some tougher early going, and how active the Castles were in charities and with the opera and all that, someone had done some digging into the dark Castle past. The story traced the family back eight generations to when the early Castles had wrested the place away from the Indians. The story even mentioned the mysterious disappearance of an early settler who had claimed an equal right to the property. While the story did not say the Castles had done away with him outright, it left the possibility open to the reader's imagination.

"Whew," Esbeth said. She put the paper down. There were hints of all kinds of pirates and blackguards in the Castle family tree. Esbeth had heard that there is often a crime behind every fortune, but to judge from the article, there was one every generation or so in the Castle clan. The paper had danced a light toe-dance right up to the edge of libel, but had backed off with just the barest amount of journalistic boilerplate to keep the paper out of the courtroom.

If Margo was incensed, Esbeth could barely imagine

how Win was taking the media's spin on the story. She hurried to take a shower and get dressed.

On the long drive out to the vineyard she turned on the radio and got a rehash of the story, along with the news that Castle Hill wine was selling out at all the local grocery and liquor stores. "There's no accounting for the public's response to a story," she thought. But at least there was some silver lining to the mess.

Within a mile of the vineyard she could tell the place was under siege. Vans were parked along the road, and two of the sheriff's department cars were handling the traffic. Esbeth was waved through by a tired looking Chunk Philips, but had to stop the car and explain to another deputy while news crews rushed toward them. When she came to the delivery entrance, she saw Boose's truck parked just inside, blocking the way. All three of his dogs were tied up in the shade beside the truck. Spook Daddy and Whitey seemed to recognize her and quit barking, but the other one, the one Boose called Bitch Dog, seemed to be trying to pull loose and attack.

Boose hopped into the truck and backed just enough to let her past. He pulled back into place and then got out and came over to where she had paused.

He did not look like he had slept all night.

"It's a regular damned circus out here," he said. There was more joy to the statement than made sense to Esbeth. But then, Boose loved a good tangle.

"A couple of those media nuts even tried to climb the deer fence," he said. "But you remember how I rigged up that old crank telephone's insides to the fence that time the coons were climbing over it to get the grapes?"

She did not, but she nodded anyway.

"Well, I gave those fellows a crank or two that'll save some of them money spent on a permanent. Their hair'll be curled for weeks."

Esbeth tried not to think of the public relations consequences of that. She nodded toward the house. "How's it going up there?"

"You just have to figure how everyone was before," he said, "and then crank that up a notch. It's loonier than the Saturday morning cartoons."

She drove on toward the house. She got out of the car and went into the tasting room before going to the house.

The first surprise was Kyle leaning against the marble-topped counter talking with Pearl. His back was to Esbeth as she entered. Esbeth caught part of the conversation as she crossed the room.

Kyle waved at the heads of deer, elk, and other heads of dead animals across the tops of the walls of the high-ceiling room. "This was all Dad's doing," he was saying. "He had us fighting over trophies for as long as I can remember. I never understood why, but it's all clearer now."

Pearl was busy counting the cash drawer before the business day began. Her lips moved as she counted, but she seemed to be giving Kyle her attention.

"Cassie called. Did I tell you that?" he said. "She wants to get back together, thinks I'm good for money again. I put her off, though. She still doesn't know about…"

"What're you doing here?" Pearl said to Esbeth, louder

than she needed. Her face was a shade paler than usual, but she was otherwise as much aglow as ever.

Kyle spun and saw Esbeth.

"I'm not here to work today. Margo called and asked if I could butt in and help the Texas Ranger," Esbeth said.

"How?"

"That's my sediment exactly."

"Don't you mean sentiment?" Kyle said, and smiled.

"She knows what she means," Pearl said.

"Yeah, there's plenty enough sentiment around here already," Esbeth said. She thought Kyle looked as relaxed and confident as he had in a long while.

"They may want you to work, after all," Pearl said. "We're expecting huge crowds today. You know, the idle curious."

"I'd hate to see anyone miss a chance for a huge marketing moment," Esbeth said, then said to Kyle, "Oh, I'm sorry. I shouldn't have…"

"No," he said. "Don't apologize. I agree. I tried to shut us down for the day. But I don't have that kind of clout, yet."

"Well, I'd better get to the house and see what Margo had in mind," Esbeth said. "Is everything all right with you, Kyle?"

"I felt bad all night," he admitted. "But I feel better out here talking to Pearl."

Esbeth watched the girl's pale cheeks turn pink. Lord love a duck, she thought. A romance on top of everything else.

In all her seventy-two years, Esbeth had not been without dealings with men. She had long ago made a study of the ways they lied, and found them much the same as the way women lied. The best technique for her was to hear the man say something she knew wasn't true, like the time Floyd Vance told her he had gone to the county fair by himself, when she had seen him with Rachel Ferguson. Esbeth had gone home crying, but she had been rational when they talked next, and listened to the way he spoke while she knew he was lying to her. There was the tiniest bit of hesitation to his words, as if he was reading off a script he had prepared. There had been an emotional tic or two, as well, just enough to barely nudge a lie detector. It wasn't something she had been able to take with her and apply throughout her subsequent dealings with men, but it had put her on the track of what to watch for, and she couldn't help but feel that Kyle was being straight and honest in everything he said. It was too bad too, because, given the competition Win had stirred up between the boys, Kyle was the number one suspect in his brother's murder.

She heard the crunch of gravel in the parking lot outside, and said, "Sounds like your first customers, Pearl."

Esbeth glanced out the windows to the lot and added, "Oh, dear."

"What is it?" Pearl asked.

"It's Cassie," Esbeth said. "I guess you didn't put her off too well, Kyle."

Kyle's hand lifted off Pearl's and zipped back across the counter. He turned to face the doorway.

Cassie marched across the parking lot and came through the doorway. Esbeth was thinking that if flames could shoot from the nose of a female, they would certainly be doing so now.

Cassie was a stunningly beautiful woman, blond and tall, like a model. But in the same room with Pearl, her beauty paled, because Pearl's beauty came from some inner depth and warmth, the kind an expectant mother gets, the translucent kind that shows through the skin. With her dark hair, pale peach-tinted complexion, and more peaceful approach to life, she was more than a match for the tanned and aggressive-looking Cassie.

"What's going on here?" Cassie snapped.

"What do you mean?" Kyle said, the lying tone Esbeth had been looking for earlier showing for the first time.

"I mean her." Cassie pointed at Pearl. "You know what I mean."

Kyle was searching for words, but Pearl wasn't. She came out around the end of the counter and faced Cassie. "You moved out the minute you were back from Belize," she said, "and Kyle already has the papers from your lawyer. You were in a world-pace heading for divorce until Chaz's death, you blood-sucking gold-digger."

"How dare you speak to me at all." Cassie's skin flushed red from deep beneath her tanning-room-browned face.

"I've talked to farm animals before. I guess I can talk to you." Pearl's fingers were curling, ready for anything Cassie could dish out. Esbeth figured that growing up with all those brothers gave Pearl the heavy edge. Cassie might have a mouth on her, but Esbeth doubted if she had the left or right punch to back it.

Cassie spun to Kyle. "Is that really the best you can do?

I mean, the woman's been in the crisis center because her husband was abusing the kid."

Pearl's voice got low and sinister. It took on a meaning and intensity Esbeth had never heard from her before. "Collin was physically abused by Rory, not sexually abused. That's why there's a restraining order on Rory. And you're a bitch for stooping low enough to even mention that. Don't you ever let mention of my son come from your mouth again."

The face of neither woman was as pretty as before. They took the first circling steps toward each other, then surged at each other, and Kyle stepped between them just as they did.

Pearl stopped and took a step back, but Kyle had to put both hands on Cassie's shoulders and move her back to prevent her from grabbing at Pearl.

"Dad's changed the will again," Kyle said.

Cassie looked at him again. She stopped struggling. "He did what?"

"Chaz's kids will get everything."

"What?"

"He told me, and even showed me the changes when he sent them over to the lawyer."

"Why would he do that?" The discussion of the will had stopped all her animosity toward Pearl. All that no longer seemed to matter.

Esbeth could think of one reason for the changes. Win thought it was Kyle who had killed Chaz. At the same time he was trying to make the law and the reporters quit poking around in the case, he suspected Kyle the whole time.

Cassie's arms dropped to her sides and Kyle's hands lifted from her shoulders. She half turned toward the door. She was thinking, adding up sums in her head. "Wow, that was fast of him. Well, I guess we're back where we were," she said.

"I guess so." Kyle risked a look over at Pearl.

But Cassie paid them no attention now. She spun and went to the door, crossed the parking lot quicker than before, and was in her car peeling out while Kyle moved over and put an arm around Pearl's shoulders.

Esbeth figured they needed a minute or two. She left the tasting room and crossed the courtyard. When she opened the door to the house and went inside, Margo, Win, and Macrory all stood facing each other in the center of the living room.

Win looked over at Esbeth. "What're you doing here?"

"I asked her to come," Margo said.

"Why?"

"To help us."

Win spun, his eyes angry and red. "Get out," he said.

"Me?" Esbeth looked at Macrory and Margo; each was as surprised as she was. Macrory raised an eyebrow, but turned to look at Win at the same time Esbeth fixed on him.

"Of course, you. Did you hear me? Get out. I won't have an old crow like you around here like all those hyenas out at the gate, sniffing around after...God knows what."

"Win," Margo said.

But Esbeth had turned and was headed toward the door. Margo came rushing after her.

Esbeth was through the door and starting across the courtyard before Margo caught up.

"I'm so sorry," she said.

Esbeth kept her feet moving.

"Wait. Wait." Margo huffed and moved faster until she was beside Esbeth.

Esbeth stopped and turned to her. "I realize you have a lot of grief in the family. I understand that. But I won't be talked to like that under any circumstances. Wake me up and have me drive fifty miles out here for that. No, Margo. Good day."

She turned and hurried around the tasting room and was halfway across the parking lot when she heard footsteps running after her.

She spun, "I said…" But it was Ranger Macrory, and he ran well for a man of near middle age.

"I was hoping to talk with you," he took deep gasping breaths once he had caught up to where she stood. "This saves me a trip to your place."

"I'm glad someone could benefit from my coming out here."

Macrory glanced back toward the house, saw Margo standing just outside the door looking their way. "Mr. Castle was telling me this morning about being the one who introduced Black Angus into Texas. I saw them out on the rest of the spread before I went to the house today. The cattle just looked at me with their tongues hanging out, like they knew it was going to be 104 degrees today too. What kind of man brings black cattle to a place where the sun beats down like it does here?"

"I think you just got a piece out of the Whitman Sampler back there," Esbeth said.

"Let me ask you, Esbeth, you know the family and the players better than me. Someone was able to get close enough to Chaz to hold his head in one of those barrels when it was opened and then was able to lug him up that ladder and try to set up an accident. Who do you figure for it? Kyle? Clive Abramson? Bill Markley?"

"That's one way it could have happened."

"What do you mean?"

"I had a lot of time to think on the long drive out here. Your way assumes he came across the sulphur dioxide where it's usually used."

"But, what else…"

Esbeth waved a hand at the sun that was already starting to beat down with its usual late summer enthusiasm. She had picked out the only tasteful black outfit she had for the kind of day she had expected, a pants suit that was just a bit heavy to be outside. She felt a trickle of sweat starting to makes its way down between her shoulder blades.

"I mean, you're talking about a gas. Wouldn't it be the lightest thing in the world for someone to carry that up the ladder, someone Chaz would let close enough to him to spray him with it. From what I hear a strong dose right in the face would be enough."

"How would anyone do that?"

"The best way I know is with an atomizer. Anyone whose ever been around perfume knows about one of those. You squeeze the bulb and it sprays."

"Good lord." Macrory looked back at the house, then at Esbeth.

"If I was you, I'd be crawling around in that Dumpster over there, or looking around on the grounds, up and down the vineyard rows, for any fresh sign of digging. You might even get something this time with a fingerprint left on it."

SEVEN

AFTER ESBETH'S CAR pulled away, with only a rising red cloud hanging in the air to mark its progress, Tillis Macrory tossed his suit jacket into his car and rolled up his shirt sleeves. Even standing in the half shade, beside where his car was parked, he felt a drop of sweat on one temple running down from the band of his hat. He walked out until he was past the grafting shed and warehouse. The sun was in the center of the sky and he cast very little shadow.

Okay, I just killed Chaz, he thought, and I'm in a hurry to hide an atomizer. But I don't want to go far, so I'll have some kind of an alibi. He looked over at the Dumpster, then went to it, climbed up the side and dropped in, crawled around inside and poked through broken wine bottles and the debris of the vineyard. There was nothing here but garbage—*basuda,* the help would say. His hopes had not been high in the first place. It was hot in here, and the place stank. He climbed back out of the big green metal container and brushed at his khaki slacks. Whew.

What was he doing out here? Years of police and investigative training and here he was out in the hot sun following the hunch of some wizened and rounded white-haired lady. But no, what he was famous for was results, the best conviction rate of any Ranger. He had gotten there by taking whatever path it took, accepting help where others would have bulled it out in silence. If this was what it took, fine.

He walked out to the edge of the rows of grape vines. With the vines up this way, the ground could be tilled to keep the soil dry and prevent the plants from getting root rot. Boose had explained all this to him, but added that the fields had not been tilled since Chaz's death. There would be footprints. Or, more likely, the person would walk along the edge of the grass along the untilled soil until an ideal place was found. He did the same, looking along the exposed reddish-brown dirt beneath the vines. A couple of times he thought he spotted Indian arrowheads, but the bits of rock turned out to be just a piece of flint or two. He wondered about the newspaper story he had read about all this being Indian land once.

He was trying to picture those Indian fighting days again, ones in which the Texas Rangers had played a significant part before they became an investigative arm of the state's law enforcement. Then he saw the little patted-down mound of dirt tucked close in to the shadow beside the root of a grape vine. It was close enough to be reached from where he stood on the grass. No footprints showed. But someone, or something, had buried something here. He hoped he was not about to find some nut a squirrel had cached. Macrory squatted down and reached over with a small grape vine twig and began to make his miniature archeological dig. Even though he half expected it, the first bit of glass made him start. The sun caught its broken glittering edge and it shined among the crumbles of dirt.

He took out his handkerchief and put all the pieces into it, careful not to touch any of the surfaces that might hold a latent print.

THE HISS OF THE teapot lifted Esbeth's head from the book she held. She got up and turned off the range, draped a tea bag into the small brown pot, and poured hot water over it. She glanced at the clock on top of the stove. It was a quarter past eight. Outside it was just getting dark in serious after another long hot Texas day. Still, it was good to be indoors enjoying the air conditioning. The days of giving tours at the vineyard had helped with the electric bill, but she would just have to cut back on something else. Heaven knew she could stand to eat less. Ever since she had retired from teaching she had become a chronic snacker. Being at the vineyard had kept her hand out of her own cookie jar, but it looked like that pastime was at an end.

The phone rang just as Esbeth was easing back into her favorite wing chair. Damn. She set the cup of tea onto the table beside her book. She got up slowly. It rang again. "I'm coming," she said. "This isn't the expressway."

She caught the phone by the kitchenette on the third ring and lifted the receiver.

"You were right."

"Who is this?" she said. "If this is someone talking about Nixon, it's kind of late to let me know."

"Sorry. It's Tillis Macrory, the Texas Ranger. Do you remember now?"

"Sure. What was I right about?"

"I found the atomizer."

"Well, I'll be… There was one?"

"You sound surprised. It was your suggestion to hunt for it."

"Yeah, but that was just a far-fetched idea so we wouldn't leave any possibility out. I guess this rules out any outsider or professional, too."

"At any rate, I did find the damned thing, even if you weren't sure it existed."

"Well, jolly good for you. Any fingerprints?"

"No." The animation in his voice over the phone waned a tiny bit. "But there's something almost as good. Someone just took a shot at Win Castle."

"And you wanted to see if I was home, not out on some grassy knoll with a sniper rifle."

"Of course not."

She hesitated, worked any enthusiasm out of her tone. "Did they get him?"

"Whoever it was didn't entirely miss. They clipped Win on the temple. He's at the hospital, and he's going to be okay."

"That's going to throw his drinking off."

"I'm more concerned with how it ties to Chaz's death."

"I take it that your assumption is that whoever shot at Win was trying to hit him."

ESBETH HAD BARELY cradled the phone, got back into her chair, and was lifting her book with one hand and the cup of tea in the other when the phone rang again.

It took four rings this time before she could get back

over to the phone. She snatched it off the cradle in mid-ring and snapped into it, "Yeah, what is it?"

"Oh, um."

"Who is this?"

"Um, it's Margo."

"Oh." Esbeth was not in a mood to make it easy for her.

"I want to apologize again, for Win, and, well, for everything."

It did Esbeth a little good to hear the normally suave Margo flustered. She waited.

"Esbeth?"

"Yeah, still here."

"We're…we're really a mess out here right now. Win's in the hospital."

"Detox?" Esbeth asked.

"No. Someone shot at him. He's not hurt bad, but they want to observe him overnight."

"Well, they're welcome to that."

"Maggie's here. She's been asking after you."

Esbeth didn't say anything.

"We both wanted to know if you'd be kind enough to come back out here and work at your regular time, day after tomorrow. We're swamped with people, and representatives of the media show up from time to time. It's all Kyle and I can do to deal with them and try to soften the awful things they try to get us to say. That Texas Ranger's out here too. He says glowing things about you. Please, Esbeth, come back. Win's being stubborn about this, the way he can be. But I'm determined to do everything in my power to find out who's behind all this. Maggie, Kyle, and

I will do everything we can do to back you up. Please come out."

"Well," Esbeth dragged the word out, "I guess I could come out and work. I've never minded that. And I can look around a bit, if I keep my head down. That's the way I work anyway. You can tell Maggie I'll do that for you. But if I seem in the way, or the law or Win wants me gone, I'm out of there like a speckled bird. I'm too old to take sass, from anyone."

"I guess, in fairness, that's all we can ask of you." Margo sounded as contrite and as genuine as Esbeth had ever heard her speak.

Esbeth hung up and thought a minute. She said, "Damn. If this keeps up I might even learn to like that dragon the littlest bit."

CHUNK PHILIPS WAS back at his station at the living-room door the next morning and ushered Clive Abramson in. Clive looked around in the living room, though he had to have been in there a number of times before. Macrory sat on the couch, his notepad in hand. He waved to the sofa where Clive had sat the last time they had talked.

Abramson was younger than Macrory, but he was no teenager. Still, he was a much more stylish dresser, Macrory noted. He was big on quality clothes that stressed texture, and he had the thin build to wear them to maximum advantage.

Clive sat down, but did little to hide the resentment on his face. "I thought we'd been through all this," he said.

Macrory looked at him. Perhaps the snappy dressing was to draw attention away from the face. Clive had a face closer to that of a weasel than probably did him good.

Macrory leaned forward and hit the button on his tape recorder. "How did you feel about losing your position as sales manager?"

"I told you all that before."

"Pretend I forgot."

"I didn't like it." His eyes were cold and direct before he looked away to flick at an imaginary speck of dust on one sleeve.

"But now that Chaz is gone, has there been any attempt to make Kyle the assistant winemaster and move you back to your spot?"

"Not so far."

"Do you think there will be?"

"I've about given up on what's going through Win Castle's so-called mind," Clive said. He glanced to the stairwell, as if expecting Margo or Maggie to be leaning out and listening.

"Is Kyle a good sales manager?"

"I couldn't say."

"Was he a good salesman when he worked under you?"

Clive sat upright from the slump he had settled into. He leaned forward. "That young pup couldn't sell hookers on a troop ship."

"And you, I suppose, could sell ice cubes to Eskimos?"

"Damned straight."

"How's all of what's happened here affect you?"

"Tell you the truth, I've brushed up the old résumé and

am sending it around. It's just a matter of time. I can sell, and I can manage."

"How did you come to be working out here? You're not particularly a young man."

Clive's head gave a small jerk. He lifted a hand to run it through his thinning hair. "You think I came out here to retire into some no-brainer high-paying job, do you? Well, you don't know much about the Castle pay scale."

"All I've noticed is a lot of tension and that there's no love lost by most of the employees here. How did you feel about Win being shot?"

Clive started to say something and stopped himself. He eased back onto the sofa and looked around the room with pursed lips. When his eyes reconnected with Macrory's, he seemed more intense. His words had a chiseled edge to them. "I'm going to say something a bit out of character here."

Macrory gave him an encouraging nod.

"What attracted me out here in the first place was the challenge. If you think it's easy for a Texas winery to make it on its own merits, then you have another think coming. It's not. It's damned hard, nearly impossible. France claimed the crown. California did everything it could to take it. Now there are only three states in America that *don't* have wine-producing commercial vineyards. Texas has at least thirty right now. Camelot Hills is bigger than Mom and Pop, but it's no Gallo, or Kendall Jackson either. Any brand name recognition it has, it's had to claw to get. It takes someone with Win Castle's drive and ruthless ambition to not only survive but to perpetuate to make it. I don't personally like the man. I think he's one economy-size asshole. But I have to tip my hat at the Quixotic spirit that drives him to try at all. I came out here with a fire in my belly to help him make it. Now I just can no longer get myself to give a rat's ass."

"So, you didn't shoot him."

Clive gave Macrory an exasperated look. He nodded toward the upstairs. "If you look around here, you'll find all kinds of guns and the heads of things that have been shot by them. But I've never once pulled a trigger, nor wished one to be pulled on anyone else."

WHEN BILL MARKLEY sat down on the sofa across from Macrory, his back never settled. He leaned forward on the edge, rubbing his hands together briskly. When Macrory hit the recorder button, Bill gave a small jump.

The man's as timid as a deer, Macrory thought. "How have things been going here at the winery?"

"Are you kidding?" Bill's eyes were open wide. "Our winemaster has just been shot at, and his son was killed before that. And whoever did it is still on the loose here. What do you mean how are things going?"

"Calm down."

Bill gave another small start. He glanced at the door, but there was no one there.

Markley was a big man, almost twice as large as his diminutive wife. Everyone else had described him as laid back. But he did not seem too relaxed at the moment.

"Where were you when someone shot at Win?"

"In bed, with my wife. We get up early to work around

here. It's only a five-mile drive, but I'm here at five, sometimes six in the morning."

Macrory kept his head down writing. "Let me get this straight. You were home, then."

"Well…"

"How do you account for the fact that you were here, dressed, and one of the ones who helped Win into the ambulance?"

Markley's eyes flicked left, then right. He looked like he wanted to jump right out of his skin.

"It must have been some other night I was home with my wife. Yeah, I was here that night. We're getting ready to start the harvest. I was testing the sugar levels of the Sauvignon Blanc and Chardonnay grapes. They'll be ready…."

Macrory held up a hand. He had noticed that Bill got comfortable every time he talked about anything to do with the physical operation of the vineyard, but that he got tense as a rabbit when he talked about people. Macrory did not want him relaxed.

"What do you think will happen to the assistant winemaster job now that Chaz is gone?"

Bill thought a moment. "I suppose I'll keep on doing what I've been doing. Nothing changed with the workload. I do as much or more than ever. I just don't get quite the same pay slip."

"You think Win will kick your salary back up where it was?"

"That sure doesn't sound like him."

"Doesn't that bother you, irritate you in the least?"

"Well, I guess it does."

"What does it make you feel like doing about it?"

"Nothing. Doing what I do out here is all I know. It was my first job out of college and I came at a time they really needed someone with my background. But I wouldn't even begin to know how to go about doing anything else."

Macrory sighed. Talking to Bill made him sorry for the whole human race. He put down his notepad and waved toward the door. "You can go."

Bill got up slowly. He was a big man, and it took him a while. He turned and started toward the door, then stopped. He pivoted back to look down toward the Ranger.

Macrory looked up. "What?"

The expression on Bill's face was hard to read—part pain, but a touch of simmering anger. That surprised the Ranger.

"When I was back in ag school," Bill said, "a fella named Joe Larry Mullins came in once and he'd been all the way in to town and had gotten himself a tattoo. He'd had a horse he cared an awful lot about, and he wanted a tattoo to remember that horse. Later he got another small tattoo about his mother, because he didn't think a horse ought to get more ink than her."

Macrory forced his eyes not to pop open wide, but he waited.

"You've got to remember, this was way back before all the tattoo craze we have today."

Macrory nodded slowly.

"Well, I thought about that a lot, long and hard. When you're spending a lot of time looking at bits of plant tissue under a microscope, you have a fair amount of time for contemplating. I tried hard to think if there was anything in my life I cared about enough to get a tattoo about, and there wasn't. It kind of made me sad, to tell you the truth. That was before I was tight with Betty Sue. You may've heard about that. We went to the same school, but didn't date until we both ended up working here. Well, my point, anyway, is that I had nothing I cared about enough for a tattoo. I've thought about murder—what it would take for someone to do that, and I've got to tell you, I have an even harder time getting to what it would take for anyone to care about enough to kill another person. Whatever intensity, madness, drive, or whatever it takes, I don't have it, and I'll thank you to quit looking down at me because of that. Do I make myself clear?"

Macrory nodded. It was the first bit of steel he had ever heard in Bill Markley's voice, and it had surprised him as much as it pleased him, though it did not help him with his case, or make him feel any better about himself either.

Markley turned back toward the door. He took his first steps, his shoulders showing just a bit of sag, when Macrory called over to him. "Let me ask you one more thing."

Bill stayed pointed toward the door, just his head swung to Macrory. "What?"

"You've had time to think about it now. The tattoo thing, I mean."

"Yeah?"

"Would you get a tattoo now? Anything you care about that much, now that you've met Betty Sue?"

Bill's head tilted an inch to the right, and he did not answer right away. Then he said, "Well, I might. I just might at that."

MACRORY TOOK SLOW STEPS up the carpeted stairs. He could hear Margo and Maggie's voices, talking to each other from behind one of the closed doors.

Margo had insisted that he feel free to poke around the house as much as he needed. An invitation is as good as a warrant, and he and Sheriff Watkins had gone through all the guns in the house, but found none that was a .22 caliber and had been fired. But there were one hell of a lot of guns in the house.

He opened the door to the second floor den. The head that rested on folded arms jerked up. Betty Sue looked at him, disoriented for a second. "Oh, I thought it was..."

"No. She's down the hall."

"Whew." Betty Sue reached up to brush at a stray lock of mousy hair. She shared a nervous grin. While her mouth was smiling, her eyes looked ready to cry.

"This whole thing's been a lot of stress on everyone, hasn't it?" Macrory said.

His eyes swept the room again. Two of the gun safes were along the far wall, both locked now. A low shelf of books about the history and technology of winemaking ran under the row of windows. The curtains were drawn. Light came in around their edges.

Betty Sue sat at a smaller desk that nestled against the wall. A large mahogany desk sprawled along another of the walls. Above it were the mounted heads of a bighorn sheep and a pronghorn antelope. He looked the other way. On that wall was the stretched skin of a mountain lion.

"There's always a bit of stress out here," she said. "It's why they pay us the big bucks."

Macrory smiled. He'd already looked through the books to see how much Clive Abramson and Bill Markley's salaries had dropped when Win had promoted his two sons. Betty Sue and Bill's salaries combined were less than half what Macrory made.

"Are you any closer to solving all this?" she asked. "That might lower the stress for us all a bit."

He shook his head, and was a bit surprised that nothing rattled. He thought a minute, then said, "What's this you said about everyone being a suspect?"

"Wha…who says I said that?"

"Everyone."

She relaxed a bit as soon as she saw it was a ploy to get a rise out of her. She was a small woman, with a determined tilt to her jaw. But she had sparkle, even though it was repressed at the moment. It was there all the same.

The phone rang. Betty Sue glanced at it and said, "Margo likes to get that when she's here."

It was picked up elsewhere.

He heard steps and Margo Castle's call down the stairs. "Mr. Macrory?"

"In here," he called out.

She leaned inside the doorway. Her eyes swept past Betty Sue and fixed on the Texas Ranger. He was staring at the mountain lion's skin.

"There's a call for you," she said. "It's Eldon."

"I thought all of these were endangered?" he said with a wave to the walls while he turned to reach for the phone on the bigger mahogany desk.

"Win said the mountain lion was threatening the Black Angus calves."

"I imagine the bighorn sheep was giving them hell too," Macrory said.

"He doesn't hunt any more these days. He spends most of his time now in the smaller cupola office upstairs." Margo tossed her head in that direction. "There's a half-empty case of wine up there he doesn't think I know anything about."

"That bothers you?"

Margo's eyes flicked to Betty Sue and narrowed, then she shrugged. "None of that concerns me. I just want whoever's doing all this found, and as quickly as possible."

While he started for the phone, Margo snapped at Betty Sue, "I need to see *you* outside for a minute."

It could have been a whip crack for the way Betty Sue shot up out of her chair, her face flushing pink as she headed for the hallway.

While Betty Sue was crossing the room, Margo spoke again. "Mr. Macrory."

He was reaching for the phone, but stopped. His head turned back toward her. Her face was pinker and the vein along her neck was throbbing. "When you catch whoever did this to my Chaz, who killed him, I pray to God that you'll have the decency not to take him in right away, but that you'll hang him up by his balls until he has died a bitter and agonizing death." Her mouth clicked shut and she spun and was off back out into the hallway.

Macrory went over to the desk and lifted the receiver. "Go ahead, Eldon."

"Do you recollect that bullet we dug out of the trim on the house there?"

Macrory did. He recalled in even greater detail the fuss Margo had made when they were digging into the wood trim at that side of the house with their knives while Win still lay there waiting for the ambulance. She had acted like the house would never be the same, the way they were scarring it up.

"Well, I got a match."

"Tell me everything."

"It was fired from one of the guns you gave me and asked to start a ballistics check. I just got the wire back from Ranger headquarters."

"Who?"

"It breaks my heart, but I'll be out there in two shakes to help you clamp on the irons."

MACRORY STOOD in the shade and leaned against the auger hopper. Out in the sun, Boose's workers were getting stacks of buckets out of the warehouse and hosing off the much bigger plastic crates that would be used when the workers came tomorrow to hand-pick the first of the grapes. Boose sat on the steps of the grape press watching them.

Out along the far rows of the vineyard, Macrory could see the sheriff's department patrol car coming the long way around the fields. The car crunched onto the gravel of the parking lot and rolled up until it was a few feet away from Macrory.

The door opened and Eldon Watkins climbed out.

"Howdy, Tillis. You, Boose." He touched the rim of his hat brim with an extended finger.

Macrory turned and they both walked together to stand in front of Boose.

He looked up at them. "What?"

"Hope we didn't catch you when you're working too hard," Eldon said.

Boose gave the twisted version of what passed with him as a grin. "Let me assure you, if I pull a groin muscle around here, it ain't gonna be mine."

"I got some hard news for you, Boose. That .22 bullet we dug from the trim over there came from your Marlin .22."

"So?"

"Did you shoot at Win Castle?" Eldon asked him straight out.

Boose's eyes squinted and then opened wide. "Eldon, you know me. If I was gonna shoot Win, I wouldn't use a .22, and I wouldn't miss."

"Do you have enough to take him in?" Macrory asked Eldon.

"Well, I talked with Win about it, and he suggested that I do just that."

The look that flashed across Boose's face was not one Macrory ever wanted to see in some dark alley. But just as quickly, all expression was gone.

"You gonna come quietly?" Eldon said.

Boose slowly pushed himself upright, pressing his jeans down along both thighs with his hands. "Well, I'm just liable to say a word or two along the way, Eldon. I hope that don't make you have kittens, or nothing."

Eldon went over and opened the back door.

Boose made the walk in that direction take as long as he could. He said, "You still getting the jail food from over to Whataburger? 'Cause I been meaning to try them."

"No, we switched."

"Aw, man." Boose's voice was a high whine. "Nothing ever stays the same around here."

"Come on. I've got more things to worry about than how the County's gonna feed you and your tapeworm."

"It's the perfect pet," Boose said. "Goes where you go, eats what you eat."

"Get in the damn car, Boose."

Boose lowered his head and slid into the back of the patrol car. Before the sheriff could close the door, Boose said, "I suppose you know that Win's gonna dock me for this time off, don't you?"

BETTY SUE CAME into the tasting room and saw that Pearl was busy. She waited until Pearl was done ringing up a case of Semillon for an older couple, who looked like drinking wine was all they had left. When they left, the frail, white-haired man barely able to carry the case, Pearl and Betty Sue were alone.

"Looks like you're going to have to take inventory again," Betty Sue said.

"But I just did." Pearl looked tired enough to cry. Her complexion was paler, and had none of its usual sheen. "And I was up all night with Collin. He had something wrong with his stomach and couldn't keep food down."

"Orders from the head dragon lady," Betty Sue said. She

gave a nervous glance back across the courtyard toward the house. "I guess there're a few tiny things missing she doesn't think should be."

"Like what?"

"Oh, Pearl, you know how she is. I don't even know if that's what's bothering her. She's all upset and lashing out in all directions. You have it far better out here, let me tell you."

"But I…"

"Just go through the motions," Betty Sue said. "Don't make me out to be the rock, or the hard place."

"I understand," Pearl said. "It's why they pay you the big bucks."

"Don't kid yourself that I make all that much more than you, kiddo. But talking about money, aren't you and Kyle getting a little friendly?"

Pearl's eyes opened all the way wide. "Oh, I hope Margo doesn't know."

"I'll tell you what you should do," Betty Sue volunteered. "Don't wait on him to be the assertive one. I should know, married to Bill. You've got to do the steering. What I did with Bill was accept. He just looked puzzled, and the only thing left for him to do was propose."

"It's nothing like…oh, my gosh." Pearl was looking out the window and saw Margo coming across the courtyard with an expression like she wanted to bite something, or someone.

"Gotta go." Betty Sue shot out one door just as Margo stormed in another.

"I came to talk to you about Kyle," Margo said, loud

enough to be heard all the way across the tasting room. She continued to click across the tiles in a rush toward Pearl, who flinched and took a step back from the counter.

Margo stopped and glared across the top of the marble at Pearl. "Is there any truth to it?"

"I…I really need this job, Margo. Please don't…."

"Then you keep it in mind. There's to be nothing between you two. Do I need to be more clear?"

Pearl shook her head, her cheeks flushing dark pink all the way back to her ears.

Margo spun and started back toward the door. She paused at the door and gave Pearl another glare. "Put it out of your head. It isn't going to happen, at least while I'm alive."

THAT EVENING, Esbeth was doing up her dishes in the sink from an early dinner. She wanted to take her book to bed so she could be up and rested for the long drive out to the vineyard.

The doorbell rang.

"Now who in Sam Hill…"

She dried her hands and went over to yank the door open. Macrory stood there.

"Do you have a moment?"

Esbeth waved for him to come inside.

He pulled over a chair from the table where she dined and sat on it near the wing chair he could tell was her power spot.

When she'd settled into it, she said, "Please tell me you have the whole thing wrapped up."

"Sorry," he said. "But things have been perking right along."

"In what way?"

"I talked with Clive Abramson and Bill Markley today."

"How did those chats affect your investigation?"

"Not at all."

"I didn't figure they would."

"And we arrested Boose."

"Oh, land's sake. You have been busier than a bee in a basin. And doing all the wrong things, too."

"Arresting Boose wasn't my idea. Win pushed for it, and Eldon went along."

"I don't know that I want to be around when Boose gets loose."

"Me neither, for that matter."

"What did you run all the way into town to talk to me about?"

"I've been through that whole bunch a couple of times now and I've gotten nowhere. I had to come in to my office anyway, to mull over what I had, which wasn't much. It occurred to me to research you a bit more."

"You think I might be a killer?"

"No. You know better. But you do hide behind that crankiness of yours, and you pull it like a cloak over yourself too much."

"I'll work on my manners."

"What I'm trying to get to say is that I found you'd been pretty sharp in those other cases where you helped out."

"Do you think?"

"But you were hampered by being around the kind of

lawmen who don't like finding out that a little old lady is sharper than they are."

"I'm not so little."

"You know what I mean." Macrory looked frustrated, but could be the soul of politeness. "What I want to know is do you have any suspicions about who's behind this?"

"I have ideas."

"I wish you'd share them."

"Young man, I admire your spunk, and you're a bright fellow besides. But I already made one mistake in something I told you earlier. Any lesson you learn is going to stick a whole lot better if you pick through the threads to this yourself."

"I don't want to learn. I want a quick solution."

"That, in a nutshell, is the problem with the world these days."

Macrory had to take two or three deep breaths this time. "Do you know, or don't you?"

"I'm in the same position of any able person interested in justice. But my hunches need evidence before I start lipping off. I suppose you're the same way before you start making arrests or taking shots in the dark."

He sighed. "Okay, so let's do this your way. But my problem is I've got a whole sewing box of threads this time."

Esbeth grinned. "A good teacher knows when to give a tiny nudge now and then."

"I could sure use a nudge now."

"Let me ask, then. What kind of thread do you think Boose is?"

"He's more of a piece of rope."

"You see, Mr. Macrory. You don't really need my help at all. You just need to think over what you already have."

IT WAS A LONG DRIVE out to the vineyard from Esbeth's place. The light slowly faded to black as Macrory drove. When he'd asked Esbeth about it earlier, she had said, "I like the long winding drive out that way. The farther I get out into the country, the more people have time to wave, from lawns as well as from other cars and trucks. I usually drive at just under the speed limit, so back in town you'd think, from the way folks act, that I was going as slow as death on the installment plan. But in the country, people have more time. I like that."

Macrory liked that too, but he was not as pleased about all the time that had gone by since the case began. The drive out did give him a chance to think over what he had so far.

First he had a killer who had to be able to get close to Chaz, who would think of an atomizer to poison him, and who had motive and opportunity. Since finding the atomizer, he had taken a second hard look at all the women around the vineyard. He had heard lots of motives from the men and the women, and not a particularly good alibi in the bunch.

Then he had someone who took a shot at Win, who may or may not have wanted to kill him. But, say they did want to kill him, why? As far as motive went there, he had even more people stacked up with reasons to hate Win. But who was there at night? He had agreed with Esbeth and did not put much stock in Boose for it. He wondered, too, what Esbeth had made a mistake about when talking to him earlier.

There was no one out this late, and the other vehicles on the road were masked by their headlights, so he could not tell if people waved as Esbeth said. But he did spot three deer at different stretches of the road. He slowed down each time, but just saw their big eyes looking back at him. None tried to run in front of him.

When he got near the vineyard, he stopped a quarter of a mile up the road, eased his car over and turned out the lights.

He took the flashlight out of the glove compartment and put it in his jacket pocket. He turned off the dome light, got out of the car, and closed the door quietly. Then he started down the road toward the vineyard.

It was quiet out. A few clouds drifted across the half-full moon. He heard the scurry of some small creature and started to reach for his flashlight, but stopped himself. He could see the dim shadow of a possum, raccoon, or armadillo moving up from a ditch to slip across the road. Contrary to popular opinion, he thought, not every armadillo is born dead beside the road. Hell, if he was out here on this case much longer he was going to start sounding like these people.

The gate was closed and locked when he walked by, and the tall deer fence had also kept reporters and others out. The only way in was the opening at the back driveway. Macrory walked even softer as he got closer.

The dim shadow he saw upright by the gatepost justified his caution. He reached and eased a pair of handcuffs out of his back pocket and took a few more soft steps.

He could see it was a man now. The man was far enough inside the gate that his back was to Macrory, and he was looking over toward the house and other buildings.

Macrory ran forward and had one cuff on a wrist before the man knew he was there. But the man bolted forward and ran down the driveway that went along beside the Chardonnay vines. The other cuff was snatched out of Macrory's hand, but he ran too, and was faster. He leaped and tackled the man, and as they rolled to the dirt of the driveway, the man's pants slid down to his knees.

He shoved Macrory to the side and tried to jump up and run, but his pants tripped him and he fell. Macrory spun him around and gave him a short punch along the side of one jaw that snapped the man's head in a jerk. He crumpled into Macrory's arms.

"That wasn't so smart," Macrory said to the crumpled dark form, as he got to his feet and brushed dirt off his clothes. "Now I've got to carry you."

The man was still unconscious, handcuffed, and locked in the back seat when Macrory pulled over at a Mom and Pop grocery that was closed. A half phone booth made of wood stuck out at the side of the building. Macrory made a call and got back in the car.

Sheriff Eldon Watkins was in street clothes when Macrory got to the sheriff's department building. Macrory led his prisoner in and Watkins started laughing.

"Who do I have here?" Macrory asked.

"Why, that's Rory Abrams. He used to be married to

Pearl. But there's a restraining order on him. He's a worthless piece of carpet filth. But I'm surprised you caught him. He's a quick one. He's outrun me twice."

"His pants fell and tripped him," Macrory said.

"Is that right?" Eldon grinned and waved toward his office.

The three of them went inside. Macrory settled Rory into one of the straight-back chairs and sat in another between Rory and the door.

Eldon tilted back in a short leather chair that squeaked. "What do you have to say, Rory?"

"I ain't saying nothin'."

Macrory started to speak, but Eldon held up a hand. He lowered himself until he could cross his arms on the desk. He looked right at Rory and said, "You probably heard, I got Boose Hargate back there in a cell. I might could let the two of you be cellmates. How's that suit you?"

Rory almost shot to his feet, but Macrory had a hand on his shoulder. He saw how wide Rory's eyes were as he eased him back to his seat.

"I heard all about that," Rory suddenly chattered. "It's why I thought it might be safe to go have a look around the place out there. Pearl wasn't to home and it was hard to figure where she was. So I was thinkin' maybe she was seeing someone out there. You know what I mean."

"Well, I'm glad you decided to be talkative, Rory. I truly am. Now tell me how your pants came to be undone enough to fall down on you like that?"

Rory lowered his head, muttered, "Nothin'."

"I mean," Eldon said, "when was the last time you had sex?"

Rory looked up. "You mean *with* someone?"

Eldon and Macrory could not help laughing. When Eldon stopped, he shook his head. "Well, son, I got to tell you, I always thought you was dim enough to think that the Mexican border pays rent. But this time you set a new low. That vineyard land is posted. We got you on trespass, violating a restraining order, and, if that wasn't enough, you just made yourself a murder suspect besides."

EIGHT

"I'M GLAD YOU'RE BACK," Maggie said.

The wholesome, young face Esbeth had hoped to see full of cheer after the wedding was touched with shadows and was full of sadness. The family had just returned from the funeral in time for another business day. Pickers were carrying their buckets through the fields, filling the larger plastic boxes with Chardonnay grapes to bring them over to the scales. Then it would be into the auger hopper and on to the crusherstemmer for the grapes. Bill Markley was hustling around, making up for the time spent in an uncomfortable suit, while Chaz had been lowered into one of the family plots far sooner than anyone could have expected. They were short-handed, with Boose still in jail, and Win back from the hospital but spending most of his time in the house.

Esbeth and Pearl were behind the tasting room counter getting ready for the day's visitors. There were always good crowds, and the tours were more fun on harvest days. But the cloud of gloom that hung over the vineyard was still there for the regular staff.

"We're so sorry for the way Father was to you," Maggie said. She crossed her arms, then let them drop to her sides, pensive, as if uncertain about what to do with herself.

"People in grief are always allowed a bit of understanding," Esbeth said. She was thinking that it would be nice if Win had been the one to deliver the apology in person. But just after the funeral, she figured Win and Margo were still in shock, the kind which that sort of ceremony engenders. She continued pulling the corks from a couple of bottles of red wine, hoping they would have time to breathe before any of the visitors showed. Bottles from the previous day were usually kept stoppered behind the counter, but all the bottles of red wine that had been open had disappeared. Esbeth had an idea who the gremlin was who had taken the bottles from the tasting room. But she wasn't going to point a finger at Win. She remembered the old saying, "Tell the truth, and it shall set you free."

"With all this publicity, we're selling wine like we never did before," Maggie said. "There's no accounting for people. But even with all that, I think Dad would rather the whole thing blow over and we got back to the way we were before, or as close to it as possible. It's Mother who's fired up to find whoever killed Chaz." The sadness swept across her face again. "Well, I've got to get back inside. Mother wants to be alone, but I'd like to be handy, if you know what I mean."

"I do." Esbeth waited until Maggie had left the tasting room and was halfway back across the courtyard before she turned to Pearl. "What's going on with you and Kyle?" she asked.

Pearl was just closing the cash drawer after counting the money. Her face flushed with highlights of pink as she turned to Esbeth. "I guess I can't hide anything from a detective like you."

Esbeth suppressed a short snort.

"Truth is, we just like talking to each other, have for a long time. He was kind when I was having all that trouble with Rory, and I've been alone a while now."

"And?"

"Since Cassie left, I've been with him a couple of times."

Esbeth didn't have to probe that to understand what Pearl was saying.

"He gets along great with little Collin, and, Esbeth, I've got to admit that he's a world-class kisser."

This time the snort got away from Esbeth before she could stop it. "Does Boose know?"

"I think he suspects. He's a pretty sharp guy. I hope you don't think…oh, Esbeth, you have the most awful expression on your face."

"I'm sorry. But at my age folks value the companionship and quality of people we're around more than if someone slips us some tongue. I didn't mean to judge, though, honey. I was young once myself, even if it doesn't look like it."

Pearl shrugged, though a couple of conflicting expressions wrestled across her face. She said, "Do you remember when Cassie showed up and wanted Kyle and her to get back together?"

"I won't forget that soon," Esbeth said. She wet the sponge by the sink and started to wipe the marble countertop.

"Well, everything Kyle told her about the will is true. Win has gone ahead and changed his will, and he showed a copy to Kyle. He plans to give the estate to Chaz's kids after all."

"Is that right?" Esbeth stopped to think. "So poor Kyle's really out of the picture, eh?"

"He doesn't seem to mind now, as much as people think he should. Cassie called and said he ought to fight Win, that that's what the old man wants. But you know Kyle. He said he wasn't going to, and Cassie changed her mind for good about coming back."

"Which you didn't mind."

"I didn't say that." Pearl looked down. "I wouldn't wish unhappiness on anyone."

It was quiet in the tasting room for a minute or two, just the squeak of the sponge Esbeth was using, the sound of some cricket that had gotten inside and was chirping from behind one of the cardboard cases of wine, and, outside, the sound of a mockingbird calling from out between the rows of grape vines. Esbeth picked through her words carefully before she spoke.

"When you were growing up around all those boys, Pearl, did you ever have occasion to hunt yourself?"

"Do you mean, was I able to kill something with a gun, or someone?"

Esbeth felt herself blush to the roots of her gray hair. Here she was, an advocate of the idea that every person is as good and as smart as another, given any opportunity, and then she was the one patronizing the likes of Pearl, about whom she cared more than she was able to describe. Esbeth had had a fair number of fatuous moments in her youth, but this was the most silly and lame she had felt in a long, long time.

But Pearl had a forgiving nature too. She said, "I used a gun, if that's what you mean, and was able to kill a squirrel or two before I got out of the notion of killing things. But before I got feeling too uppity about the whole idea, I had to think hard about buying any kind of meat, even fish, from a grocery. Someone had to kill it, and by eating it I was just as guilty. I never got caught up in the idea, though, that it was worse to kill anything, from a dolphin to a baby seal, just because it was a degree smarter or cuter than some pig or steer."

Esbeth sighed. "What I meant…"

Pearl interrupted. "Something you don't know about is how our Daddy died. He shot himself. He used a shotgun, pulled the trigger with his toe. There was some talk about how one of us might've helped him, lord knows he was sick enough at the time, had cancer bad. Boose or one of the others would've had the guts for that, but they didn't do it. Daddy done it himself. I don't know why people had doubts; they never did about Hemingway when he done the same thing. But anyway, Esbeth, that's really when I was done with guns, and with killing, if you want to know."

Now Esbeth felt small enough to walk out under the crack of the door without bothering to open it. "I'm sorry," she said. "Sorry to bother you about any of this."

OUTSIDE THE PICKERS WERE emptying their buckets into the big plastic tubs and the tractor was bringing those over to the scales for weighing, when the first cluster of visitors arrived inside the tasting room and Esbeth called out, "How many of you would like to go on a tour?" They all held up their hands.

Esbeth organized them into a group and led them out the door, feeling that first charge of excitement at being back. She liked giving the tours, especially the talking and then giving out free tastes of the wine. It was a lot more social than her quiet times around her house.

She took them over by the auger hopper and told them about Win and Margo's romantic trip to France so long ago, and how it inspired them to start a winery. When she got to the part about the process she turned and pointed out the auger hopper. It was a big stainless steel tank, with sturdy sides that rose four feet up from the cement; and it was eight feet wide by twelve feet long, with insides that tapered down to a narrower base where a steel auger—a foot wide and looking like a giant screw of blades—lay along the middle.

"We work in volume around here," Esbeth said. "It takes eighteen pounds of grapes just to make a single bottle of wine. They'll pour tons of grapes here into this auger hopper which channels the grapes over at the rate of eleven tons an hour to the crusher-stemmer—that gadget there that's replaced the jumping up and down on the grapes, taken all the fun out of this business, and…"

There was a squeal of tires, sliding gravel, and a crash out in the parking lot. One of the ladies in Esbeth's group yelled, "Oh, Fred, that's our car."

Pablo, one of Boose's workers, was driving the fork lift and stopped beside the auger hopper. His head spun and he hopped off and went running toward the parking lot. The whole crowd eased that way. Fred and his distraught wife were in the lead. Esbeth shrugged and went with them. It was bright out in the sun, and she could see the pickup truck that had backed around wrong and slammed into one of the parked cars. The door to the truck opened and Betty Sue popped out, still in her nice clothes from the funeral and looking as rattled as Esbeth had ever seen her. She looked around, didn't see Bill anywhere, and she went running toward the house, through one door of the tasting room and out the other, then shot across the courtyard and went inside the door.

A few more people who had just arrived came out of the tasting room to join the crowd. Esbeth went closer to the wreck with them. She couldn't believe how much damage had been done. Fred and his wife were taking turns shouting at each other and looking toward the house. Pablo got into the Markleys' truck and backed it away from the crumpled front of the Lincoln Towncar. As the cars pulled apart they made a horrendous screeching sound as the backward kiss of metal ripping apart tore bits of both cars loose to fall in metal flakes to the gravel of the parking lot. Then Pablo got out and everyone crowded closer to get a new perspective on the damage.

It was five to ten minutes before Bill and Betty Sue Markley came out, and Win was with them. The white bandage around Win's head made him look like the Spirit of '76, and he had taken off his black suit jacket and tie. There was a red smear on his white shirt, and a trickle of red from the corner of his mouth that made him look the tiniest bit like Dracula. We all have our way of mourning, Esbeth thought. He must have been up in his hideaway sampling the goods again.

It took a while to trade insurance information. Fred and his wife got a chance to shake hands with the winemaster himself, although Win could not know that he was not putting out his best appearance. When Esbeth got the group herded back together, without Fred and his wife, but with a dozen new arrivals, she led them back to find Pablo dumping loads of Chardonnay grapes into the auger hopper. It was nearly full.

"Well, we're in luck," she told the group. "I've only gotten to talk about how they process the grapes, but we might get a chance to see how it's done."

Bill Markley came over to the control panel between the hopper and the crusher-stemmer. He still looked a bit rattled from having his truck fender smashed. "Boose usually does this," he said to Esbeth, "but I haven't forgotten how." He looked out at the faces in the crowd around Esbeth. "What you'll see is the grapes being moved and torn up by the auger, then the bunches broken apart as they go into the crusher-stemmer. Centrifugal force is used inside to break the grape into 'must'—that's M U S T: the juice, the pulp, the seeds, and the skins—while the stems go up that smaller auger on the other end of the crusher-stemmer where they're dropped into the cart you see to be taken out to the mulch pit."

Esbeth had shared the story often enough, and was surprised that the usually shy Bill was so willing to talk. But if it had to do with grapes and the winemaking process, he was in his element.

"The 'must' will be pumped over to the big wine press you see over there—" he nodded toward the big cylinder that lay on its side, one of the men holding a five-inch-wide hose into it "—and it'll come out a pale-green color. Okay, here goes."

He hit the button and the auger began to churn. The grapes, already torn up a bit began to tumble out a ramp and down into the funnel of the crusher-stemmer. Pale green juice flowed out, but then turned to a bright red. Someone in the crowd gasped. Another pointed and screamed. Bill's shaking hands scrambled for the button, and he turned off all the machines. But all the people were yelling now, and the red juice still came out, running in a trickle down the ramp.

Esbeth's eyes were open as wide as everyone else in the crowd. They had all taken steps back, and some had turned and run shouting into the tasting room. She forced herself to look at everyone's face. Bill Markley turned and stared at her, his face washed white. His hands shook so bad he had trouble letting go of the control panel.

Win and Betty Sue came running out from the house; Pearl and Kyle came from the tasting room. Pablo climbed off the fork lift, and the other workers were running this way.

"Don't anybody leave," Esbeth shouted. "The sheriff and a Texas Ranger are going to want to talk to all of you."

Pearl was crying. She ran over and grabbed Esbeth. "Who is it?"

"I don't know," Esbeth snapped, pushing her way past as she went for the phone. "All we can do is call for help."

Bill and Win were in a huddle by the tasting room door.

"You might have the men start taking those grapes out of there," Esbeth said. "If someone's in there, we might be able to help them."

"But who…" Win started to say.

"I don't know," Esbeth shouted, "but you're not helping whoever it is by talking it over."

Both men broke into a run and started shouting instructions to the men while Esbeth went inside to make her call.

SHERIFF WATKINS AND Ranger Macrory had both arrived by the time members of the vineyard field staff, and the EMS crew that had arrived just ahead of the law, were able to get to Margo Castle's body at the bottom of the auger hopper. Chunk Philips was back at his station at the locked front gate. But someone had been glued to their police scanner and had picked up the call with the Castle name in it. Vans were pulling up out along the road, and two television news helicopters were buzzing back and forth taking footage of the winery from the air.

The staff and family members were huddled outside the tasting room and all of them saw the EMS workers lift the body out onto the open body bag on a gurney. What was left of Margo's mangled head tore loose from the body and fell to the concrete, leaving just the bloody stump of her neck. Esbeth could see the severed spine, the ends of veins sticking out. Most of the blood had long since poured out into the hopper. The head rolled over and came to a rest against the wine press, with one of the EMS men chasing it as it rolled. Both Maggie and Betty Sue fainted at the same moment, nearly colliding as they fell, but neither anywhere near being able to care.

Margo was no one's Florence Nightingale, Esbeth thought to herself as she shuddered, but I would never have wished this on her.

Kyle stood with his face washed as pale as Esbeth had ever seen it. Pearl openly had an arm around him, but no one seemed to notice. Win Castle stood with his mouth hanging open an inch. He looked haggard, worn, with his arms hanging down limp at his sides, and now more than ever like some Shakespearean character facing up to the worst of tragedy.

Macrory had been watching the faces in the group. He frowned, but before he could say anything, Kyle called out to the others. "Someone give me a hand getting these women inside."

He stooped and lifted Maggie. Bill Markley had caught Betty Sue, enough to keep her head from slamming into the concrete. He picked her up as easily as most people would carry a feather pillow and was already moving across the courtyard.

Though they were all in some state of shock, as the EMS workers zipped up the bag and started for the waiting ambulance, Esbeth was surprised, and a bit pleased, at the assertive side that either the crisis or being around Pearl was bringing out in Kyle.

Win followed the group that went inside, his arms still hanging at his sides and with the dull look of someone unable to see pasted across his face.

Macrory watched Pearl and the others go inside too. He

eased over closer to where Esbeth stood staring over at the auger hopper.

"You look about as off balance as I've ever seen you," Macrory said.

Esbeth shook herself. "This certainly knocks what I was thinking into a cocked hat."

"What was that?"

She shook her head. "It would take someone strong to lift Margo's body into that auger hopper, wouldn't it?"

Macrory looked back over at the four foot tall steel sides of the hopper. "It would at that."

"And I doubt if we'll ever know if she'd been hit on the head first, will we?"

"Forensics might get more than you think. If she was knocked out, or dead before she was put in there, we may have enough tissue to show us that, though it'll be a bit of reconstruction getting there."

"Who did you have picked before?" he repeated.

She gave another irritated shake of her head. "Maybe I'm just too old for this sort of thing, after all."

A car pulled up in a crunch of gravel into the parking lot and stopped. A tall man in a cowboy hat got out on the driver's side.

"Uh oh," Macrory said. "It's the boss."

The tall man walked toward them, in the rangy slow stroll of someone who has ridden horses in his life. He touched his hat with a thumb and forefinger as he gave a short nod to Esbeth, then he took a few steps away. Macrory walked over to face him.

"Well, Till, just what the hell you got going on here?"

"This one's almost got me up a stump, Lute, but I'm not feeling all the way snake-bit yet."

"I'm starting to worry you're going to run out of suspects on this one if everyone keeps turning up dead."

"Seems every time I narrow things down, something comes along that changes the whole take on a prime suspect," Macrory's glance swept from the auger hopper over to the house. "You come out to take over this?"

"You know better, Till. I'm here to watch you work, in your mysterious ways, your wonders to perform. You still have the best record of any Ranger. I'm here for moral support, that's all."

Macrory turned when Sheriff Eldon Watkins came out of the door to the house and started across the courtyard.

"They all accounted for, Eldon?"

"All except that Clive Abramson fella."

"Come over here, Eldon. I want you to meet Lieutenant Tim Comber."

"Hell, I know Tim. We go way back to a time someone was trying to rustle an emu. But that's a story we'll both save for some better spitting and whittling moment. What brings you out here, Tim?"

"Just back-up for Tillis, here. Someone's got to go talk to the press, too, and you know I'm prettier by far than this old piece of boot."

Macrory smiled. "You can have the press as far as I'm concerned." He turned to Eldon. "Can one of your men check on this Abramson guy? I guess he lives in an apartment over in that county seat of yours."

Eldon nodded and went toward his car to use the radio.

Macrory turned to Esbeth, who had been standing in the shade by the tasting room. "I guess we can start with you, Esbeth, if you like."

"And get me out of the way, and out of here?"

"You can stay on if you like."

The Ranger Lieutenant moved closer and held out a hand big as a catcher's mitt. "So you're the Esbeth Walters that Till has been telling me about."

"I hope it wasn't at the head of his suspects list," Esbeth said, shaking his big hand.

"No. He did have you down for knowing more than you're telling, though."

"Well, I don't feel like I know as much as I did. Margo's murder doesn't fit with anything I had worked out."

Macrory said, "Why don't you give Tim here a thumbnail sketch of Margo Castle."

"Well," Esbeth said, "she wasn't ever going to be elected Miss Congeniality. She was hyper class-conscious, a control freak with a capital 'C', and she spent half her time accusing staff members of stealing, anything from paper clips to lawn furniture. Margo made clear that she felt that anyone other than a member of the Castle family was of a lower cut of life. She knew she didn't have to have everyone's affection, and she sure didn't try for it."

"That's quite a eulogy," the lieutenant said. He glanced at Macrory.

Esbeth sighed. "Just about everyone around here at one time or another has said that if anything ever happens to Margo, the suspect is going to be everyone."

"That doesn't simplify your job, Till," Comber said.

"No, it doesn't," the Ranger said. "And I'm not even sure that the missing Clive Abramson will."

Eldon Watkins came crunching back across the parking lot. He was shaking his head. "The man's place is cleaned out. There was nothing in the whole apartment except an empty soft drink Dixie cup in the center of the kitchen floor, and the ice was melting in that," he told the two Rangers. "He's as gone as last Thanksgiving."

"That might help a bit," the lieutenant said.

Macrory frowned. "We'll start the usual checks on credit card activity, the works. In the meantime, let's go in and talk to the others."

KYLE AND PEARL SAT on either side of Maggie on the sofa. Betty Sue was still stretched out on the couch, her head on Bill Markley's lap.

Macrory went over to Betty Sue. "How're you feeling?"

"I'm…better, I guess." She started to try and sit up, but Bill tugged her back to the horizontal.

Bill looked up at Macrory. "Go ahead and ask her questions from here, if you've got to," he said.

Macrory eased down onto the corner of the coffee table. The furrows in his forehead were a bit deeper than usual. "What were you up to when you had that fender-bender in the parking lot?" he asked.

Betty Sue hesitated, looked up at Bill. "Margo had sent me on an errand. She'd gone in the kitchen and found they were all out of coffee. She went into one of her fits about how someone had to rush to the store and get it right that moment." She looked up into Bill's eyes. "You know how Margo can get when she wants something."

Bill nodded. He looked at Macrory and said, "But you don't have to take our word for it. Ask Miss Maggie or Kyle, if either of them are up to it."

"So, you were flustered," Macrory said.

"I was. And as much as I thought I might even feel better some day if Margo wasn't yelling for one thing or another, I feel more flustered now." Two streams of tears started down both sides of her face, and she turned her head away and grabbed Bill around the waist.

"I understand," the Ranger said.

Macrory turned slowly on the end of the coffee table until he faced Kyle and Maggie. Pearl sat quietly on the other side of Maggie. "Where's Win?"

Kyle gave a nod upward.

Macrory turned to his lieutenant. "Go up there and bring him down before he's too incoherent to talk." He made the sign of tilting his thumb to his mouth.

Lieutenant Comber turned and started up the stairs. He came back down ten minutes later, leading Win Castle down the stairs of his own home. Win looked liked someone who could not have found the way on his own. His face was a puffy blotch and the only thing holding him back in his progress while upstairs had been the need of a funnel. From under his white head bandage, his red, bloodshot eyes flicked around the room and settled on Pearl.

"What's *she* doing in here?"

Kyle stood up and said, "Dad, for once in your life, just

sit down and shut up." Each word got louder as he spoke until he was nearly shouting.

Win blinked at him, but said nothing. He went over to a chair in the corner and lowered himself into it.

Lieutenant Comber came over close to Macrory and bent to whisper in his ear, "Win tried to order us and the sheriff off his property. I had to threaten him with being jailed himself."

Macrory nodded. He turned to Pearl and said, "By the way, Sheriff Watkins is bringing your brother back to the place. His truck's still here."

She nodded. "Good. His dogs are a tough lot to feed."

There was a tap at the door. Win had sat up straighter in his chair when he heard Boose was being set free. At the tap he was all the way to his feet.

Macrory looked over at Win. The man was an absolute mess—haggard, staring, and hulking around the place with no care for his personal appearance. He was beginning to resemble a madman. But hell, he'd just lost his wife, right on the heels of being shot himself and losing his heir.

Lieutenant Comber got the door. It was Howie Upwood. He introduced himself and shot around the couch until he was down on one knee beside Maggie.

"Are you all right?" he said.

"Mother's dead," she said, the words coming out like a hollow echo.

"I heard. How are *you* doing?"

"Maggie?" Macrory said.

"Yes?" She looked up at him.

"You were supposed to be keeping an eye on your mother. Did she get away from you?"

"Oh, you've got to know my mother. She flits around. She was in her room, then down to the kitchen and banging around. She yelled for Betty Sue about something, probably the coffee, then I didn't see her for a while. I was up in my room changing. Oh, my God. Do you think I had something to do with her being murdered? Oh, if I'd just stayed right beside her." She broke into hysterical tears and Howie reached to pull her closer.

Macrory stood up. He would question Maggie more later. It sure seemed Maggie and Howie Upwood's early shot at happiness was having a rough time of it.

He said to everyone in the room. "Has anyone here seen anything of Clive Abramson all day?"

They all shook their heads.

"Anyone know where he might go if he was to leave here for any reason?"

There was a low murmur of them talking to each other, but no one volunteered any information.

Win shouted, "Do you think he's the one who did this?"

"We don't know what to think, just yet," the lieutenant said. "But when we have anything fit to share with you, we will."

Macrory and Comber both moved over closer together by the door and were talking in low tones to each other. Win Castle came across the room toward them. "Don't let that man out," he pleaded.

"Do you mean Boose?"

Win nodded.

"There's no way he did anything. He has the best alibi of anyone at the moment," Macrory said.

"You've got to keep him locked up." Win looked at them with pleading eyes.

Kyle stood up. "Dad. You're not making any sense. Go dry up. Talk to Pablo and the others. Bill, you might as well go, too. We've got to decide what to do about today's harvest. As soon as the officers are done with the auger hopper we need to super-clean it and handle the rest of the grapes or all that's a loss. And, Dad, we aren't opening the tasting room tomorrow, or the rest of this week for that matter. But Pearl, Esbeth, and the others can come out and help somewhere. We won't stiff them out of their paychecks."

"Later," his father said. "We'll talk later."

"Oh, no we won't," Kyle said. "We'll do it this way. Just sit back and try not to think right now. It's not going to be your strong point for a few days, so don't over-do it."

Win's head bobbed back in a half-drunk weave. His mouth opened, then shut. He turned and walked down the hall toward the connecting hallway to the lab and barrel room. Bill got up and followed him.

Pearl was looking up at Kyle with a pleased expression on her face. Maggie was looking at him differently too.

Macrory and his lieutenant slipped out the door onto the courtyard. "You know," Macrory said, "I believe that Pearl's beginning to be a good influence for Kyle. When I first got out here, I wouldn't have given you a nickel for a dozen of him."

"He looks good to me, too," the lieutenant said. "If you didn't have a man missing, he'd be your number one suspect."

MACRORY AND COMBER were in the tasting room talking with Esbeth when the sheriff's patrol car pulled into the parking lot with Boose in the passenger seat.

Boose got out of the car and started walking toward the back of the winery buildings.

"Oh, my," Esbeth said. "That looks like a man on a mission."

"Where do you suppose he's going?" Macrory said.

The Ranger ran over to the door and yanked it open, but Boose was gone. Eldon Watkins was walking across the gravel over toward them.

"I'm going to go talk with all the field hands," Comber said. "I might even see if any of the migratory pickers saw anything. You see if you can get that Boose to come help me. I speak the lingo, but he no doubt speaks it their way."

Macrory called over to Eldon before he was all the way across the parking lot, "Did Boose seem okay on the ride out here?"

"Oh, he was grinning like a mule eating briars."

Macrory shook his head. "You know, with Boose, I'm thinking that him grinning isn't necessarily a good thing, depending on who he's thinking about when he's grinning."

"Where would he be headed?" Macrory asked Esbeth. She got up from the low stool where she had been sitting while she waited, and led the way out the back and over to the fermentation room.

As soon as they opened the door, Macrory could hear a racket coming from behind the closed doors at the other end. He broke into a run, and Esbeth came along as fast as she could behind him.

Macrory glanced into the barrel room, then all the way down to the bottling area. Esbeth caught up, then went over to the lab door and swung it open.

Boose was astride Win Castle, who was down on the floor. Boose held him in place and was thumping on him, first with one hand, then with the other, like a cat playing with a mouse. Win held his hands up in a feeble gesture, but otherwise made no effort to stop Boose from hitting him. Bill Markley stood with his back pressed against the lab counter, staying out of the way.

Before Macrory could rush into the room, Kyle came running from inside the house and shot across the hallway and into the lab ahead of the Ranger.

He reached and grabbed Boose's shoulder and pulled Boose upright so fast it surprised him. Boose spun and had a fist halfway to Kyle before he saw who it was and stopped. "Aw, man," he said in his high country whine, "I was just getting a good rhythm going with his head."

Win lay still on the floor, his hands halfway up as they had been. He stared up at nothing, his face already beginning to swell beneath the bandages.

"Don't you see, Boose," Kyle said, "he was enjoying it too much. What he wants right now is a good beating. Don't give him what he wants. Let him stew in his own juice for a while."

Boose turned and looked down at the man who signed

his paychecks. He looked like he didn't know whether to pity Win or kick him. Then he shook himself and brushed past Kyle and Macrory and went to stand just outside the fermentation room, muttering low to himself.

It took both Macrory and Kyle to help Win to his feet. He looked around in a dazed way. Macrory could not tell if he was drunk or punchy from being knocked about in the fight.

"Will you be wanting to press charges?" Macrory asked, more interested in the answer than the action.

"No." Win shook his head as if hearing bells. "It was just a business-related misunderstanding."

"I didn't misunderstand nothing," Boose yelled from where he stood. Then he spun and walked off through the fermentation room.

"You had better help him upstairs and put him to bed," Macrory said to Kyle.

Kyle led his father down the hallway, but before they passed through the doorway into the house, Macrory heard Kyle say, "Don't say that, Dad. You're just as responsible yourself for everything evil that's fallen onto this family."

Then the door closed behind them.

Macrory looked at Esbeth. "I've got to admit that I've never had a case that shot me in more directions than this one. What would you be doing if you were me?"

"I guess your procedure is already in place to see if you can run down what happened to Clive, isn't it?"

"Sure. But nothing from there so far. Tim thinks I could do well to keep a close eye on Kyle."

"You know, he's onto something there that very well might pay you dividends."

"What do you mean?"

"If I tell you everything, you won't ever learn anything."

"I wish you'd quit trying to be a teacher and just tell me everything you suspect. Who's behind this?"

"Things slipped and slid on me a bit, just like they did on you. All I'm talking about is following the best thread of the moment. And by the way, Kyle's car is the brown Jaguar. You might want to put one of those thing-a-ma-bobs on it."

Esbeth turned and went on out through the fermentation room herself, looking for just this once her real age.

MACRORY SAT IN HIS CAR tucked off behind a low stand of mesquite trees, half dozing behind the steering wheel. Kyle's house was just up the road a mile, and he had been keeping an eye on it, had seen Pearl's car come and go, and was glad Eldon was keeping Rory Abrams on ice at the jail.

His eyes snapped open at the sound of a car. He sat up straighter, watched the road, and saw a low car go by on the road. It was too dark to see if it was brown, or a Jaguar, but he heard the sound of the car's engine and nodded.

He reached over and turned on a small screen on the seat beside him. A ping of light went moving down the road ahead of him.

"Well, I'll be damned," he said, and started the car and pulled out to follow Kyle.

NINE

MACRORY FOLLOWED the little blip of light on the screen beside him. It led him down past San Antonio, where he pulled onto the highway heading for Corpus Christi. The night wrapped around his car like a black glove. But he still stayed far enough back that Kyle could never see even his headlights.

A night drive is a good time to think, he figured. He watched the other cars go by in the other direction, pairs of lights off to their own destinations, hard to tell where at this hour. The lines on the highway flicked by in rows of dashes that seemed to stretch into the night.

Esbeth Walters had said she liked to think while she was driving. He liked that feisty old gal. She knew enough to lay back on her oars and not push her nose too far into an investigation, but she had a natural aptitude for this sort of thing.

He was certain that she knew more than she was telling. But something had happened that made her doubt herself—probably that it would have taken someone strong to carry Margo to the auger hopper and drop her in while the crowd was gathered around the accident in the parking lot. Margo's autopsy had revealed that someone had hit her over the head first, but though the Rangers and

Eldon's men had covered every inch of the buildings, they had never found whatever someone had used to hit Margo.

Who did he like for the two murders? He had to agree with Comber that Kyle was his best bet. But first he needed to straighten out this Clive Abramson business. Why had he taken off?

The blip stopped and Macrory pulled his car over to the side of the road and stopped too. He was watching the screen when a car pulled up behind him. A Texas Highway patrolman got out of his car and came up to the driver's side.

Macrory had both hands up where the trooper could see them, though his badge was on his shirt and his white Texas Ranger hat on the seat beside him.

"Oh," the patrolman said, quick to see the signs of a fellow employee of the Department of Public Safety. "Is there anything I can do to help?"

"Is there a roadside rest up ahead?"

"Yeah, about a mile and a quarter."

"That's about right," Macrory said. "Thanks, but that's all the help I need."

The trooper went back to his car, eased out around Macrory's car, and drove away.

The blip stayed put.

After another twenty minutes, Macrory started his car again and pulled out onto the highway. When he drove past the roadside rest he could see the Jaguar pulled up in one of the parking spaces.

He drove on down the highway, trying not to pass too many exit ramps before he found a truck stop that was open. He finally spotted the bright lights of a sprawling truck stop like a nighttime highway oasis ahead at an intersection. He took the off ramp and pulled in at Bubba Leroy's Roadside Cup o' Joe. Eighteen-wheeler semi-trucks were lined up in rows, their diesel engines churning low and soft while the drivers slept inside the back of the cabs.

He was halfway to the diner when a woman in a tight mini skirt came swiftly toward him, her tank top concealing little. He held up his badge before she was close to him, and she veered and moved off in another direction as fast as her tight skirt and heels would let her.

Macrory got two tall containers of coffee in Styrofoam cups and a couple of large packages of beef jerky. He sat in his car and watched the comings and goings in the parking lot for a little over two hours, but he never saw another of the highway hookers. Perhaps the word had gone out that there was a Ranger on the lot. When he glanced away from the parking lot and looked over at the screen next, he could see that the blip was moving again.

"So, you're done with your nap, are you?" He put the coffee he held back into the holder and started his car. He waited until Kyle's Jaguar passed the intersection where he sat, gave it a few minutes, and pulled out again onto the ramp heading back to the highway.

The horizon to the east was showing a thin bright line, like a cracking egg, and the lower part of the sky was turning to a light gray as Macrory's car came over the rise of an overpass and he saw the first outlines of buildings against the sky.

The first time he had ever come to Corpus he had been surprised at the height of the skyscrapers clustered into a tight knot in the center of Corpus Christi. But oil money was responsible for most of them, and not many of them were new.

On the outskirts of the city, he pulled over again and waited to see which way the blip would take him. The sky was getting lighter and the first of the morning rush hour traffic began to pass him, headed in to the city.

The blip swung around on the outside of the city and headed north, so Macrory pulled into traffic and followed it. Once he was past Corpus, Kyle took the off road toward Port Aransas. Macrory smiled to himself. It would not be long now, he figured.

When the blip finally stopped, Macrory was still a mile from Kyle's car, but moving through the downtown of Port Aransas. He had to take a side street and then followed a row of houses and businesses that lined the intercoastal shoreline. Ahead he saw the brown Jaguar parked along the sidewalk. He pulled his car over and got out, walked the rest of the way to the building. It was the Sea Horse Inn. *So, it's like that, is it?*

He loosened his gun in its holster, but did not expect to need it.

It was early to bother the Inn's manager, but before he could even look for the office he heard the shouting coming from one of the low pink cabanas that lined the waterfront. He eased around to the back of the inn and went along a walk of flagstones that led through thick flowerbeds, all lush with marigolds, geraniums, and here and there a plastic pink flamingo.

The cabana's door had been left partially open. He eased it all the way open and stepped inside.

Kyle stood just inches from Clive and he was shouting. Clive stood with a bedspread wrapped around his waist. In the bed, with a sheet partially covering him, was a dark-skinned young Hispanic man with the smooth skin of someone only half of Clive's age. No surprises so far, Macrory figured. He knew what kind of bed and breakfast place the Sea Horse was.

"Oh, Clive," the man in the bed called out. "Yoo hoo. More company."

But Clive had already spotted Macrory, and now Kyle spun and saw the Texas Ranger too.

"Get your clothes on, Clive." Macrory was looking around the room.

"I was just asking him…" Kyle started to say.

"Shut up. You're coming too."

Everyone stayed quiet while Clive dropped his bed-spread and struggled into his clothes. He ran his fingers through his hair and looked at Macrory. "Mr. Macrory, do I have time to…"

"No." Macrory had his handcuffs out and stepped closer. He clamped one end onto Clive's right wrist and reached for Kyle's left arm.

Kyle snatched his arm back. "What do you think you're doing?"

"That should be obvious to even the meanest intelligence. Now, give me your wrist."

Kyle blinked, then held out his wrist and let Macrory clamp the other end of the handcuffs into place.

"Oh, oh. Do I get a set? Let me play," the man on the bed said.

"Paulo, shut up. This isn't a game," Clive said.

"He's right, Paulo," Macrory said, "unless you want a long ride too."

Paulo made a gesture of zipping his lip. He plopped back onto the bed and pulled the sheet up to his chin and tried to pout in as cute a way as he could.

Macrory held Clive by the upper arm, led them out to his car, and got them to slide into the back seat. He locked it on them, then went around and got into the driver's side.

"What about my car?" Kyle said.

"Someone will come and get it, or, if everything goes well for you, you might be able to come down and pick it up yourself." Macrory started the car and turned around in the street to go back the way he had come.

It was quiet in the back seat, except for a brief scuffle or two as the two passengers adjusted to riding with their wrists handcuffed together.

As they reached the outskirts of Corpus Christi and started up the highway, Kyle said, "Are you sure you know what you're doing?"

"First of all, Kyle, don't you say anything for a few minutes," Macrory said. He drove and glanced back at them in the rearview mirror as he headed north. "Clive, what were you doing, leaving the scene of an investigation the way you did?"

"I…I knew better. But it was driving me crazy. I just needed a break from it."

"The way you packed up and left your apartment

doesn't make it look like you had a short break in mind. And you were very careful not to use your credit cards. You knew we could track you that way. None of this looks very good for you."

Kyle said, "Not to mention..."

"Don't get personal, Kyle," Clive said. "I wasn't sleeping with the help, at least."

"I never had anything to do with Pearl until Cassie made it clear she was leaving me."

"But your tongue was hanging out a long time before that."

"You don't know how it was living with Cassie. How could you?"

"Maybe I know enough to avoid that whole kind of relationship," Clive said.

Macrory had let them go long enough, hoping he might uncover something. Now he stepped in. "Kyle," he said, "I said no talking, and I meant it. I'll let you know when it's time for you to speak."

Kyle turned to his window, gave his right wrist a shake when he realized he was still cuffed to Clive.

"Children," Macrory snapped, "if I have to stop the car and come back there…"

It got quiet in the back seat, Kyle staring out his window in a sulk, and Clive looking ahead, waiting.

"Go ahead, Clive. You were going to tell me why you knowingly put the spotlight on yourself by taking off," Macrory said.

"I didn't want the spotlight. I wanted out of it, and I wanted far away from anyone named Castle."

"Where were you all day yesterday?"

"Here. With Paulo. You should have asked him while we were there."

"You're probably right about that." But Macrory doubted that. He did not like Clive for Chaz's murder, and liked him even less for Margo's. There was nothing personal enough in either case to make him kill. There *was* enough to make him leave, but he should have been sensible about waiting the proper amount of time before doing that. Kyle, on the other hand, was another whole plate of beans.

"Now, Clive, you stay buttoned this time. I'm going to ask Kyle some questions. Understand?"

"Yes." It was a mutter.

"What exactly were you thinking, Kyle, driving all the way down here?"

"I knew that Clive had a place he went to when he wanted to get away. It was always the same place, even the same cabana, so I figured that's where he went when he disappeared from the winery."

"Are you familiar with the phrase, 'withholding evidence from the police'?"

"Yes, sir."

"You know I could lock you up, too. The next time you interfere with an investigation and hold something back, I will. Do you understand? It's good to see you asserting yourself a bit, but stay within the law when you do. There seems to be something in the collective Castle psychology that says laws are for other people. I want you to wean yourself of that right now. Am I getting through to you?"

"Yes."

Macrory figured that Kyle had grown up in the same ethereal air his father had, where there is little real sense of the value of money, or at least of that which has to be earned. The rules of life must seem soft to people like the Castles, the biggest frogs in their little ponds. But was that what had made Kyle mutton-headed enough to go after Clive on his own, or was he covering up for the murder of his mother too? Macrory knew that the late dame of Castle Hills would have never allowed Kyle to marry Pearl, and that just might be motive enough for her death. He didn't even have to think hard for a motive for Kyle to kill Chaz.

"What did you think you'd learn from Clive that was worth a trip down here?"

"I object," Clive said.

"You don't have the right. Shut up," Macrory said. "Go ahead, Kyle."

"I wanted to know if he knew anything. I didn't think he had murdered Chaz, or Mom. But I thought he might have seen, or heard, or known something."

"All of which is my job," Macrory said. "But as long as we're on the subject, did you know anything like that, Clive?"

"No. It was just my nerves. The whole damn bunch, sorry, Kyle…but they were making my skin crawl. One of them was a killer. I didn't want to be around at all any more."

"Who do *you* think committed the murders, Clive?"

"It's hard to say. The more I know them, the more I think any one of them is capable of it."

MACRORY SKIRTED AROUND two television station vans along the road and came in the back way at the vineyard, past one of Eldon Watkins' men at the gate. He pulled his car into the parking lot.

He was climbing out of his car, stiff from a long day and night behind the wheel—that and drinking too much coffee and eating only junk food.

The winery was abuzz with another day of picking. The tractor was bringing over the tubs of grapes to the scales, and Pablo was dumping the tubs into the auger hopper with the fork lift. Macrory saw a sight he had never expected to see. Esbeth and Pearl were both decked out in rubber aprons and oversized rubber boots. They were spraying the tubs with a high pressure hose and helping get the wine press clean for processing the different variety of grapes.

He walked up to where the two ladies had stepped back to let Pablo through to put the empty crate onto a stack and go get another tub of grapes. Pearl glanced up at him, looked like she started to say something, but stopped.

"How're you two getting along? It looks like Kyle lived up to his word in getting you different work since the tasting room's closed for a few days."

"This is different, and fun," Esbeth said, running a forearm across her forehead, "but it's tiresome work. How about you? Did you have any luck in your endeavors?"

"Yeah," he said. "Kyle's over at the jail."

Pearl dropped her hose.

Macrory turned to her. "He's just got some questions to answer, and I left him there with Lieutenant Comber. Clive's there too. We might need to talk to him a little longer."

"But neither of them's your killer?" Esbeth said.

"Esbeth," Pearl said.

"He knows what I mean." Esbeth gave Pearl a look.

"No, I don't think so," Macrory said, for Pearl's sake.

"That should narrow things right down for you."

"Um, Esbeth. Can I get you to step aside for a couple minutes? There're some things I want to discuss with you."

"Can you take over, Pearl?"

She nodded.

Bill Markley came out of the fermentation room. He was headed for the growing mound of Sauvignon Blanc grapes in the auger hopper. Esbeth pointed to herself and Macrory, and Bill just nodded. He went over to the controls and started the grapes moving through the auger hopper to the crusherstemmer.

Macrory took a few steps so they would be away from the noise.

"Don't you want to stay close and watch, make sure there's not another body in there?" Esbeth said.

"No, I don't. You're a bit macabre today."

"It must be this place." She gave a little shudder. "I can't imagine drinking a wine after Margo went through there. But you know what they say about staying out of the kitchen if you're going to enjoy eating at a restaurant."

Macrory could not help himself. He had to glance over at the hopper.

When he looked back at her, he said, "I want to know if you've got anything to say to me yet. I want to know who you suspect."

She cocked her head and squinted as she looked up into his tired and expectant face.

"You know, you lawmen fellows are starting to remind me a lot of the weathermen these days. They've got all that equipment, barometers, Doppler radar, wheels turning, machines cranking, and there isn't one of them who can tell you for sure if it's going to rain or not. They're right less than half the time."

"What's that have to do with…"

Esbeth interrupted, "And here you have tons of scientific data, forensic pathology reports, psychological profiles, and you can't sort through something so simple Watson could get it, much less Holmes."

"You didn't answer the question," he said. His teeth weren't clenched, but he was showing glimmers of more irritation than he had so far. Perhaps it was the night without sleep.

"Let me ask you something," Esbeth said.

He nodded slowly.

"Were there fingerprints on Boose's rifle?" she asked.

"No."

"Just like everything else, wiped clean, eh? And were there any powder burns on Win when they treated him?"

"How did you know about that?" His eyes opened wider.

"It makes sense. He thought Kyle was the killer, and he was trying to point a finger in any other direction. Boose looked good for it. Win managed to clip himself and leave a bullet in the house for easy finding, then wiped away his own fingerprints and put the gun back in Boose's truck. But anyone who knows Boose would know he's going to leave fingerprints everywhere. His guns haven't been wiped down even when they needed it."

"How long have you known about that?"

"Since you told me someone had shot at Win and missed."

Macrory just looked at her.

She said, "You've got to give the old boy credit. That's not as easy as it seems, shooting yourself with a rifle. He might have even had to take another shot to get a bullet in the house so it would match. But a .22 doesn't make that much noise."

"All that to throw suspicion at Boose," Macrory said.

"And away from Kyle," she said.

"Do you think?"

"I think that's what Win thought. He probably held himself responsible for pitting the boys against each other the way he did. It's hard to say how his brain works these days. He's been as stewed as a boiled owl ever since I've worked here, and that's been just since his heart attack. How did Win say it happened?"

"He said he was on his way out to check the sugar levels on the grapes. It's something they do this time of year," Macrory said.

Esbeth gave one of her short snorts. "First of all, you're describing the actions of an obsessive winemaster. Win hasn't been that since his heart attack, and has gotten even less so the more he's been drinking. We just mentioned that. Another thing, the grapes getting ripe now are the white ones. Margo encouraged them to plant the red grapes around the house, the Cab and the Merlot, because they're prettier. Do you mean to say he planned to walk to the far extremes of the fields in fading light to test the sugar levels of grapes? I don't think so. His story didn't hold up for me. I'm surprised it did to anyone else."

"Anything else you're holding back?"

"I'm not holding anything back. It's all the same stuff you know."

"But you know things I haven't told anyone."

"Yet we both still have the same cast of characters, don't we?" she said.

He sighed. "Can't you tell me something I don't know?"

"It's a shame you didn't have a big old frozen fish laying around in any of this."

Macrory's face took on a pasty hue. "What did you say?"

"A big old frozen fish. Why, did you have one?"

He said, "The day of Chaz's funeral, they were going to have one of the chars that Chaz had caught when the boys were with their father up in the Pacific Northwest on a fishing outing. That's a kind of salmon, you know." Esbeth gave an irritated nod. "Margo had taken it out of the freezer but never got around to cooking it. After she was killed, everyone was so rattled that they ended up sending Kyle to town to pick up some burgers."

Esbeth looked up at him, sad, and still a little tired looking in her rubber wet gear.

"When that fish started to smell later, it was thrown out," he said.

"Well, it's a damned shame you fellows probably thought a thing like that was too cliché to matter."

"Why's that?"

"Because that's when I think you lost the weapon that, while the fish was still frozen, was used to hit her on the head."

"That's too far for me to stretch," he said.

"Well, there's the rub, then. Everything you've had so far is like it was lifted out of some old detective story comic book."

"That's more common than you'd think in these cases out in remote country spots like this."

"So, it doesn't make anything at all more clear for you?"

"No."

Esbeth shook her head. One corner of her mouth twisted into a disgusted pinch. "Well, Officer, I don't know how you can expect me to give you an 'A' for this kind of work."

THE TWO OF THEM stood looking into the monitor screen that showed Kyle's cell. He sat on the edge of his metal bed with his chin on his fists, staring at the blank opposite wall.

"Eldon has him a pretty good rig here for a county jail," Tim Comber said.

"It's good if you like to watch people who are at the low ebb of their personality," Macrory said.

"You ever wonder, Till, if you don't have too much heart for this kind of work?"

Macrory looked at the lieutenant to see if any kind of smile was on his face. But Tim was being serious. "You think that?" he asked.

"I'm just saying…"

Tim was long and lanky, stringy like a six-foot stretch of beef jerky. Macrory was giving thought to how Tim would take it if Macrory took a swing at him. He guessed he would not like it, or understand. "Whatever you're saying," Macrory said, "you didn't finish saying it."

Comber cocked his head at Macrory, trying to see through the Ranger. Whatever he saw seemed to please him more than displease him. "You still have the best record of anyone, Till. What do you think?"

"Do you know of anything I don't, some reason I should book this guy? I mean other than his trying to be a junior vigilante. Anything like hard evidence, or something I could take to a grand jury?"

Comber shook his head, his eyes still narrowed at Macrory. The air around them was close to crackling from the tension.

"Then, what say we go talk to the prisoner?" Macrory said.

Kyle looked up at them when they came up to his cell door and the turnkey let them in. Macrory searched his face for any sign of guilt, and found none. But, damn, it would be nice to wrap this up.

"They treating you all right in here?" Comber asked him.

"Look, I don't care which of you wants to play the good cop or the bad one. I screwed up by going down there without telling you. But it's my brother and mother who've been killed here. Doesn't that weigh anything?"

"That's what points most your way," Comber said.

"But I inherit nothing. Haven't you checked on my father's changes to the will?"

"Truth is, that adds to the stack against you rather than takes away." Comber nodded to Macrory. "Isn't that right?"

Macrory nodded slowly. "It's an almost certain thing,

Kyle, that your dad thinks you killed your brother, maybe your mother too."

"But don't you need some hard evidence, something firm that points to me?"

"You've been watching too much television. You have no alibi for either death, and you had means, motive, and opportunity."

"There's a good argument against motive when you're talking about Mom's death," Kyle said. "I can't believe you take that seriously. But, about Dad thinking I did it. Where do you get that?"

"Don't you see, as screwed up as he is about his family name living on, he would do about anything to shift blame away from you right now, even if he thinks you're stone certain guilty. And he's probably blaming himself more for being the one to stir you and Chaz against each other."

Kyle lowered his head and thought a moment. Then he looked back up at the two Rangers. "That sounds a lot more like his problem than mine, doesn't it?"

LIEUTENANT TIM COMBER, Sheriff Eldon Watkins, and Ranger Tillis Macrory all sat in Eldon's office. For the better part of an hour they had been trying to make sense of the situation out at the Castle spread.

"You going to let this little old lady solve the case for you, Till?" the lieutenant asked.

"No." Then Macrory thought a moment and he changed that. "At least, I hope not. But I do like the old gal."

"Maybe if she was about a hundred years younger, you

could fit her out in a Ranger outfit." Eldon was tilted back in his chair and picking at a fleck of mud on one boot. Given the least opportunity, and being late in the day, he had reverted to the good-ol'-boy country sheriff comfort of being himself.

Comber said, "I believe I heard you telling that cute young dispatcher you had back a while ago that age is a matter of mind—if you don't mind, it don't matter." He watched the sheriff's face.

Eldon grinned. "I'd like to say that my perspective on that young heifer was different. But I guess everything's relative. The wife made me let her go, anyhow. But that Esbeth's as old as my Uncle Rum, and we're pretty sure he was a waiter at the Last Supper."

"You're certainly full of beans tonight," Comber said, encouraging the sheriff without meaning to.

"The fact is, though," Macrory said, "that this is one of those cases where all the evidence in the world doesn't matter as much as seeing through to the human heart. That old gal, Esbeth, has seen through a lot more than I have."

"If you had to pick right now, who would you finger for the two murders, Till?" the sheriff asked.

"I thought I was down to Kyle, or that Bill Markley," he admitted.

"But not Clive at all?"

"Your fellas pinned down his alibi on Margo's death. That Paulo guy may be a butterfly, but he hasn't any reason to lie for the likes of Clive Abramson."

"You figure Clive run just 'cause he got antsy?"

"I'm just surprised more of them haven't," Macrory

said. "The only thing holding the rest back is they're all related to someone out there. It's a tight little bunch, but you got to remember that dynamite being wrapped tight is what makes it have a kick."

"And Win Castle is doing more to trip us than help us," Comber said.

"He's sure full of himself," Eldon said, "and when he's had a glass or two, he can be meaner than turkey turd beer."

"He *is* a loose cannon," Macrory agreed. "We might as well turn Kyle loose back there and stir up the mix, see what that gets us."

"I agree," Comber said. "You're at an impasse. Someone's got to light the fuse, even if we take a bit of risk."

"I'll have one of the deputies load him up and haul him out there. Let him figure out how to get his own Jaguar back from Port Aransas later. It's the kind of challenge a young man with money needs."

"You never said why you think Bill Markley might be good for it," Eldon said.

"Just a process of elimination. Hell, it's no worse than voting for a national president—picking the lesser of evils," Macrory said. "I have about as much to go on in this case."

"Pitch it to me," Comber said.

"Yeah," Eldon said, "and make it good. I haven't ever in my life had the media pressure I'm getting on this one. They're more than hinting that I oughta step down and let someone handle this who knows what they're doing. I come up for election again next year, so give me a hand here, boys. Hell, I'm just laughing to keep from crying."

When Eldon was done spouting, Macrory said, "Okay. Bill Markley lost the most by all the shuffling around out there. He got a salary cut and was demoted."

"But wasn't all that fixed by Chaz being killed?" Tim asked.

"It might've been, but Win's been in such a state that he never got around to putting things back the way they were. Maybe in the conniving way his head works, he didn't want to reward a killer for bumping off his son. Maybe he's just being tight-fisted, which fits with him."

Eldon nodded a confirmation. "But do you think Bill has what it takes to kill one, maybe two people?"

"No," Macrory admitted. "But that moves the fickle finger to Kyle. Since he's been seeing Pearl, he's either found his spine, or grown one."

Eldon gave a low whistle. "Can't fault him much. I'd as soon watch that girl walk as eat fried chicken."

Macrory gave him a short frown, but erased it almost as quickly. "What I have a harder time figuring is what she sees in him."

"A woman's love is like the dew," Eldon said. "It's as apt to fall on a horse turd as a rose."

"I suspect it has more to do with helping him ease out of whatever rut he was in," the lieutenant said.

"Well," Eldon said. "You're talking about the human heart, and that gal's sure captured his heart, as well as a few other organs, no doubt. What do you think?"

Macrory said, "I think it was a mistake for us to have left Boose here in jail as long as we did, given the way it's affected your speech."

"Go ahead," Tim Comber encouraged his Ranger. "Tell me again. What makes Kyle our target?"

"I figure it took a man to be able to lift Margo and put her in that hopper. That's four feet off the ground, and though Margo might've weighed one-twenty at most, I can't see a woman getting her in there. Then too, Win had those two boys whipped into a frenzy about who was going to inherit the place. Kyle's the smarter of the two boys..."

"If brains were leather," Eldon butted in, "that Chaz wouldn't have had enough to saddle a flea."

Comber said, "Can you spare us some of that for a moment, Eldon? Go ahead, Till."

"I was just saying that Kyle's the thinker. We're stymied, and it's because whoever's behind this has outthought us all along the way. These murders are the work of someone who either thought everything out well in advance, or they were extraordinarily lucky along the way."

"How're you gonna arrest Kyle, though, if you have no evidence, like you say?" Eldon scratched his stomach and stared at Macrory.

"The only way I know is a bit of slack rope. Turn him loose out there the way we're doing and have one of us or one of your men around the whole time."

"All I can tell you," Eldon said, "is that if it was me out there, and I knew the killer was loose in our tight little circle, I'd be as nervous as an old maid in an asparagus patch."

The lieutenant sighed.

Macrory looked at the clock on Eldon's wall. "Well, I'd better get over to my motel and rest. I have the daytime shift there tomorrow. Maybe we'll have some luck and get this wrapped up before the media starts howling for *all* of our resignations."

IT HAD BEEN a long day at the vineyard. The sun had been down for several hours when Bill and Betty Sue Markley climbed into their truck and headed for home. Boose was walking over toward his truck, and Kyle called to him, "Did you finish up that chore I asked you to do?"

"I sure did." Boose grinned. "Pearl's got the only key." He hopped into his truck and was not far behind the Markley truck going down the far lane.

Kyle turned and Pearl stood waiting. She looked tired, and pretty.

"You didn't have to wait here on me," he said.

"I wanted to make sure you got home. I called a sitter to pick up Collin from the day care. But I've gotta go now."

"Why don't you stay for just a few minutes and come inside."

"Are you sure?"

"They're going to all have to get used to you sooner or later."

They went into the house. Maggie and Howie sat on the couch and were bent over the coffee table looking over a photograph album. Maggie's eyes were rimmed with red, so Kyle knew they had encountered quite a few pictures of Margo and Chaz. In the far corner of the room, Chunk Philips sat in the wing chair frowning down at a copy of the oversized *Wine Aficionado* magazine. It was not his kind of reading, apparently, but it was all there was in the living area to look through.

Maggie still wore a tasteful black dress. Her face seemed paler than usual against the black. Howie looked up from the album as Kyle and Pearl settled in the sofa across from them. "I haven't had the chance to see you since you got back. How was it in jail?"

"They didn't put me in a cell for keeps," Kyle said, sounding a little disappointed. "But they did chew me out for withholding information and for going after Clive on my own, even if I did lead them to him."

"Was he..." Howie glanced at Maggie, then back at Kyle. "Is he the murderer?"

Howie had a long, slightly freckled face under sandy-reddish hair. He wore a suit jacket over an open collar and seemed in sharp contrast to the working people who had been swarming around the winery all day.

Kyle said, "They didn't act like they thought he was, though it's a little hard to tell what those cop-types think." Chunk Philips lowered his magazine.

Maggie looked up, and she appeared ready to say something, but instead she glanced to the stairway, where Win was coming down, and hanging onto the railing in an exaggerated way. His face was flushed red and still puffy with bruises under the white bandage, and though he wore a different shirt, it too now sported a wine stain.

He stopped three steps from the bottom. His head swayed as he looked around the room, and his glare settled on Chunk Philips in the corner. "What's he still doing here?"

"Eldon Watkins stationed a man here. There'll be someone around the clock until all this is cleared up and settled," Kyle said.

Win's bandaged head slowly panned until it came to Kyle and Pearl sitting together. "I thought I told you about her. Get her out of here."

Pearl started to jump to her feet, but Kyle put a hand on her shoulder and slowly stood up, facing his father.

Chunk put down his magazine and was watching the scene with as much interest as he would have shown "Monday Night Football."

Kyle and his father glared at each other.

Howie cleared his throat. "She seems to come from good pioneer stock," he said. "Perhaps your blood line could do with a good infusion of that."

Win's head reeled back a wobbly inch, and his glare shifted to Howie. "I'll thank you to butt out of Castle business, since you'll never be one and are responsible for my daughter no longer being a Castle."

He ignored Maggie's shocked look and pointed a finger at Kyle. "You have a responsibility to the Castle name, and that includes not sporting with the likes of…of that." His finger shifted to Pearl.

Pearl struggled past Kyle's hand and stood up. She shouted at Win, "I won't be talked about like that."

Maggie's voice was softer. "We won't be either."

Pearl yelled over at her, "Shut up, Maggie. What your father's saying about me is far more serious, and nasty."

Maggie collapsed in tears onto Howie's shoulder. He looked over her hair at the Castles as if they were something that had climbed out of the moat.

Pearl pushed around Kyle and ran for the door, opened it and went through to the courtyard, slamming it behind her.

Kyle rushed after her, but he stopped at the door and glared at his father, "What responsibility you've had, you've faced as a drunken sot, and now you've lost a son and a wife because of it. So don't you preach to me."

Win staggered and had to grab at the rail. "Don't talk like that. I did everything I could to get someone else to take the fall. And why? For you."

"That was another alcoholic mistake, Dad, because I didn't kill anyone, and if you could draw a sober breath, you might see that."

He looked at his father, swaying and blustering. Mad as he was, it tore his heart in two to see that there were no teeth in the old lion.

Maggie's sobbing was the only sound in the room. Chunk Philips still leaned forward in his chair watching. The tension in the Castle home was as great as it had ever been.

Kyle turned and opened the door to go after Pearl. But first he said back over his shoulder, "You be careful, Dad. I mean it. I hold you responsible for everything that's happened here. If you keep this up, you're going to get just what you want."

Then he went out the door with another bang.

Kyle came back in a few minutes later. Outside there was the sound of a car with a spin of tires in the gravel.

Win had gone upstairs. It was just Maggie and Howie in the living room beside Chunk Philips, who had gone back to his magazine.

Maggie looked up at Kyle with bloodshot eyes. "Howie and I are going to take off first thing in the morning," she

said. "We need to get off and pull our lives together without all this." She waved a vague hand toward the upstairs.

"Maybe Dad's right," her voice quivered. "I'm not really a Castle anymore. And for once, that feels like a good
thing."

TEN

"Esbeth Walters!"

Esbeth got out of her car and looked over to her neighbor's house. It was Mrs. McCorkle, sticking her bony head out around the corner porch post. She was waving a piece of newspaper.

"What?" Esbeth yelled. She was darned if she would give that coot the satisfaction of trotting over there.

"You're in the paper again. Messing around where you shouldn't, no doubt."

"Humpf," Esbeth muttered to herself, and got her packages out of the car and headed for the house. It was her day off, and nearly noon at that.

"And selling liquor, it says here," McCorkle waved the paper hard enough to make a brisk rustling sound.

"It's wine," Esbeth yelled, "and I just give tours. Anyway, prohibition's over." Under her breath she muttered, "You crusty old dingbat." Then she added, "And so's the Depression. Read that part of the paper."

Esbeth went inside and had to put the packages down before she could go back and slam the door behind her.

"I'm getting old," she said to herself. "I should have had all this on a plate for that nice Ranger by now. I thought I had a good handle, but…"

She let it trail off, busied herself with opening the box she had so lovingly carried. She lifted out an apple pie big enough to feed a logging camp. The top crust rose to a rounded and browned peak four inches above the edge of the pie pan. The inside would be filled with the best granny smith apples, brown sugar, and all manner of calories. The smell of the still-warm pie lifted up and nearly made Esbeth swoon. There was only one place near her that made pies from scratch this way, and that was at Carol Bean's Mean Baking Machine, a tiny shop just two blocks down the street. Esbeth had made herself quit visiting there for a few months while she sought to kick her sweet-tooth habit. But this was a crisis.

She cut a piece from the pie and put it on a plate, then went to get the teapot boiling. All of her best thinking usually came while she was doing something else, something familiar, whether taking a bath or driving the car. But this time she felt she needed the stimulation of eating a piece of a Carol Bean pie.

When she had a cup of tea ready, she sat down at her small dinette table. There were a lot of things she should be doing, ranging from cleaning the house to catching up on the news herself. She glanced over at the paper she had brought in, but didn't reach for it. She doubted if there was anything there to clear up the current muddle, and she had seen her own name in print before in connection with murder investigations.

She lifted her fork and cut off a perfect bite of the pie. She was lifting it to her mouth when she stopped. "Oh, shoot a bug," she said. She dropped the fork and the bite back onto the plate and hopped up out of her chair. Esbeth snatched the keys off the hook by the door, locked the house behind her, and hustled to the car. "I've been so dense," she said, and started the engine and backed down the drive. "I should have seen that all along."

THE DRIVE OUT to the Camelot Hills winery was no longer than usual, but Tillis Macrory took his time getting there. He spent some of the time looking out across all the cattle spreads he passed, even pulled over and stopped the car at a blackened stretch where a brush fire had swept to the road and had turned at least a hundred acres into a scene from the other side of the moon. The grass, which had been yellow, was gone and only blackened ground remained. Clumps of prickly pear cactus were twisted into gnarly yellow fists with thorns sticking out like pincushions.

Macrory got out of his car and smelled the charred mesquite and sage smell. The fire had swept three to four feet up the trunks of the mesquite trees, turning the trunks black. But the grass fire had been so quick it hadn't caught the trees themselves on fire. Two trucks were parked along the road up ahead, another far behind him. A man in a volunteer fireman's jacket walked up along the edge of the road toward the Ranger.

The fireman nodded his blacked face when he got close enough to see the badge on Macrory's chest. The car's antenna, search light, and Macrory's white hat had already given him a clue. He said, "Some asshole threw a cigarette butt out a window. Every car I've ever been in has an ash tray, and we've been telling folks for weeks we've got drought conditions here. But this is what you get." He waved an expansive hand at all the black and walked on down the road toward his truck.

Macrory stood a while looking at the scorched earth. Nature was odd that way, but an occasional burn was good for the land. In a while, hunters would be coming around here too, knowing that deer can hardly resist coming to new growth for a feed.

Seeing the black, desolated moonscape that this piece of some Texas spread had become should have left him shocked and hollow. Instead, all he could think about was that he would sure like to have a cigarette right now. Damn. He had not smoked a cigarette in almost eleven years. He could have kicked himself.

He got back into the car and started off again. For some reason he was thinking of his ex-wife, Claire, instead of the Castle family and the two murders on his plate.

Every now and again, there comes a clarifying moment in your life, he thought, where in a burst you try to decide whether your life has been a failure or a success, whether everything you've been doing is toward something or just a lot of busy work. The moment may have been ripened by the recollection of all the stumbles you made, stacked beside the pitiable mound of what you call successes. He couldn't even say if he felt he was failing with the Castle case, or not. It certainly had a dimension or two that defied standard procedure and pure logic. He had told Tim Comber that he felt a little snake-bit. For the first time he began to wonder if there hadn't been more truth to that than he thought. Maybe some of the Castle poison, the self-doubt and irrational squirreliness of Win Castle, was starting to rub off on him. He shook his head and drove a bit faster.

KYLE PUT DOWN his razor and leaned closer and looked into the mirror. He wiped away a streak of shaving cream and looked into the eyes that stared back at him. He had been expecting some kind of change, something new there.

He threw water on his face and reached for a towel. For the past day he had been thinking about the lush greenness, the sea-saltiness of the tropics. Belize was in far contrast to the dust-covered dark green and pale yellow of Texas at this time of year. But this was home. It felt so, and had always been so.

But with Chaz dead, and his mother as well, there were disoriented moments when it seemed he was on another planet. Cassie was gone too, for that matter. But there was Pearl. She was his anchor now. Kyle had lived so long in the assurance that all this would one day be his that he had never seen how much of that was Cassie's dream, not part of his. With Pearl, all that was different. They were just two people, able to care about each other. No matter what happened—the whole Camelot Hills estate could crumble—they would still have what they had.

"WHO'S BEEN UP in my cupola office?" Win's face had settled into patches of purple bruises from the beating he had gotten from Boose. He hadn't changed the bandage around his head. Macrory stood leaning against the wall. From his vantage point, Win looked more crazy now that he was sober than he had when he was drunk. Win's head was tilted a bit to the right and his hair stuck out from beneath the not entirely white bandage. His eyes were flicking around the room, and he looked as demented as Macrory had ever seen him.

"If you mean the wine, Dad, I'm the one who took it out of there," Kyle said. He and Bill were up on top of a fermentation tank, while Boose was below, hooking up a pump. Macrory was way down past the end tank. He'd been at the vineyard an hour by now and was mentally clicking through the list of suspects again.

Win Castle's gray head tossed like some wounded lion as he glanced around the room at the others. Even Boose, who he had ordered around for so many years, was busy ignoring him.

"I had Boose change the locks on the tasting room too," Kyle shouted down at his father. "We even locked up all the wine we keep in reserve for topping off barrels. You need help, Dad. Don't make us institutionalize you."

"We'll see about that." Win looked over at Boose, who gave him a maniacal grin back.

"I wouldn't try ordering Boose around just now, if I were you."

"Why do you defy me?"

"Because I love you. I want the father back I once had, not the blurred and shambly one that's let all this happen to us, has caused half of it."

"Oh, I've caused all this, have I?"

Kyle nodded, too sad for words.

"It's her that's caused this in you, isn't it?"

"Do you mean Pearl?"

"I sure as bent pluperfect hell do."

"Then I need to thank her." Kyle was glad Pearl was locked in the tasting room taking inventory where she wouldn't have to hear Win spout off during his involuntary sobering up period.

Win's head moved in bird-like jerks as he glanced around the cool fermentation room. His hands clenched into fists and unclenched again.

"I've heard often enough from you how it was with you and your father," Kyle yelled, "how you practically drove your own father out the business when he got older. He died not too long after that. Maybe you didn't kill him outright, but you broke his heart. If that's what you're waiting on from me, you've got a long wait. I swear I'll never do that to you. Believe me on that."

Win's expression looked painfully sober. He hesitated, then looked up at his son and shouted back, "You make me glad I left the place to Chaz's kids. Maybe they'll grow up with some of his spunk."

"That wasn't spunk, Dad. You made him into a minor thug."

"Yeah," Boose said. "He wasn't worth a milk bucket under a bull."

Win spun on him. "You shut up."

Boose looked like he was ready to jump up and have another go at Win, but Kyle held out the flat of his hand to Boose. "He's half out of his head, Boose. Don't give him what he wants. Remember?"

Boose eased back down by the pump, looking like a dog who'd just had a bone yanked away.

"I'm glad you changed the will, Dad. If running this place the way you think it needs to be run turns me into what you've become, I don't need that. But don't forget that I love you. I want you to get well."

"I'm not sick, you impertinent pup." Win's voice was as close to a snarl as the human voice can get.

Win looked like there was a lot more he wanted to say, but he glanced over at the Texas Ranger and spun and stormed back out, closing the big metal doors to the barrel room, lab, and bottling area behind him.

"Well, he sure took off like a duck in a hailstorm," Boose said.

"I...I should be more supportive for the next few days," Kyle said. "These are going to be tough ones for him. I'll go try to calm him down after a bit. But he'd better have a few moments first."

"I can tell you," Boose said, "that there're two people I want to be able to forget someday, and he's both of them."

Kyle frowned at him.

"He won't do anything wild, will he?" Bill asked. "He looked a little crazy to me."

"Where's Betty Sue?" Kyle asked.

"In the office, doing what she always does."

Kyle nodded. She was just up the stairs a flight. If Bill needed to check on her, she was handy.

The Ranger had been just thinking that it wouldn't take too much at this point for one of them to slip and show more of his hand than he wanted to share. The tension out here at the winery was as high as he had ever felt it.

A long time back Macrory had had to force-feed himself on the idea of patience. All that made him think of the feisty little Esbeth Walters. As his knowledge had evolved, it had led to knowing just how little he really knew, and that had helped make him become a better watcher and listener.

Being out here, standing around without doing anything, could either be the biggest waste of time he could be making, or it could be exactly what he needed to do. He did feel closer to the end, without knowing exactly why.

He had been looking around the fermentation room and had spotted a two-wheel cart he had never noticed before. Someone could have used that to haul an unconscious Margo through the house, out through the connecting door, and out through the fermentation tank toward the door where the auger hopper was outside. But it still would have taken someone strong enough to lift her hundred-twenty-pound body up over the four-foot stainless steel edge, wouldn't it? Boose had been in jail, and Win had been upstairs knocking back wine in the cupola office. Between Kyle and Bill, who did he like best? Well, neither of them, for all that.

The door to the outside opened and Esbeth Walters stuck her head inside, looked around until she spotted Macrory.

"We aren't running tours today, are we?" Kyle called down to her.

"No. I just came out to have a word with the Ranger here," she said. "I haven't punched in, or anything."

Kyle laughed. "I'm not the one who worries about that."

"Keep an eye open while you're here, though," Boose said. "Win's roaming around here somewhere like a wounded buffalo. He's one of them people who think reality's for people who can't hold their liquor."

Esbeth nodded, though she had a puzzled frown. She went back outside and Macrory followed.

"What was all that about?" Esbeth asked him when they were alone and leaning on the railing by the crusher-stemmer. She consciously stayed several feet away from the auger hopper.

"Kyle's trying to dry out his father enough to get the old boy to see reason. I know all of this has been stressful, but I suspect his drinking problem goes back to before all this happened. What do you think?"

"Win's weakness while trying to bring out strengths in the boys isn't my problem right now."

"I know what you mean. There're a lot of places I'd rather be than here right now."

"Think about me," Esbeth said. "I just abandoned an entire untouched Carol Bean pie."

"What?"

"Look—" she glanced at the door "—I came out all in-a lather because I know now."

"You know who did the murders?"

"I've known all along. I was just too brick-headed to get myself past the speed bump of one detail. But now that makes sense too."

"It was Kyle, wasn't it?" Macrory said.

"No. Of course not. How could you even think that?"

"It was you suggested that I follow him. Why would anyone do such a lunk-headed thing as go to Corpus Christi after Clive if he wasn't trying to cover his own guilt? A normal reaction would be to just tell the law where Clive usually went, something Kyle knew and kept from us."

"You've got to understand that Kyle's head, at his advanced state of being freshly in love, is fairly mushy in spots. I'll tell you my guess about why he felt compelled to ride down there like some kind of Lochinvar and bring Clive Abramson back. He hadn't done anything in all the time he'd known Pearl to distinguish himself, to win his spurs with her, so to speak, and he probably thought this was his big chance. The deaths of his brother and his mother would have him off-balance; being encouraged to be more assertive by Pearl just iced that cake."

"And you saw that coming?"

"Not specifically, but I knew he was due to do something daffy that smacked of knight errantry. I could see it in the vacuous determination of his face."

"Well, I didn't," Macrory said.

"You wouldn't have."

"It wasn't Kyle, then?"

"That's what I've been trying to get through to that sun-baked Texas Ranger head of yours—hat you maybe should've gotten onto yourself when Margo was killed."

"Well, don't keep me in suspense." Macrory leaned closer. Anyone else might have been annoyed at the disrespect Esbeth was showing him. But he had been through too many turns on this case to care much about that right now.

"What's that?" Esbeth said, tilting an ear up to listen closer.

"What's what?"

"You hear it? Shouting. From inside."

She rushed over to the door and swung it open. They could both hear the yelling, and Bill was hurrying across the fermentation room toward them.

"I was just coming to get you," he shouted to Macrory. He turned and started running. He swung open the double doors at the other end of the room and left them open. Then he ran around the corner into the barrel room.

The shouting was distinct now, two voices, Win's and Kyle's.

Esbeth and Macrory arrived outside the open sliding door to the barrel room at the same time. Inside was a scene that might have fit better in Dante's *Inferno*. Kyle stood shouting up at his father, who was scampering across the barrels. Wine ran down across his shirt and from the corners of his mouth. He held a partially filled bottle and the tasting syphon he had been using. Boose was right behind him, trying to grab him.

"Be careful, Boose. We just want to get him, not hurt him," Kyle yelled.

Boose gave a not very reassuring, "Hee, hee, hee."

Bill Markley eased back out of the room and stood beside Macrory and Esbeth. "Kyle caught him up on one of the barrels that was nearly done aging," he explained.

Win gave a hop and Boose slipped at the same time and fell sideways down onto a rack of the barrels. Win spun and doubled back, just beyond Boose's reach. The thick oak barrels were held in place by metal frames that were swaying and crashing together from the men tumbling and running around on top. Each of the barrels held almost sixty gallons, and most of them in this room were full.

Boose was scrambling back to his feet, the sinister grin he sometimes wore was spread clear across his face. Win ran to the far end and leaped, landed on his feet on the concrete floor, and tumbled forward. The bottle he had held crashed, and broken glass and red wine covered the floor around him. Bill rushed into the room for the first time to help Kyle try and hold him down.

Kyle and Bill were bent over the fallen Win, then were suddenly pushed back in a rush when Win rose like a madman possessed and threw them both back.

Boose leaped through the air at Win, who ducked to one side just in time. Boose smashed into the other side of barrels, and the already swaying stacks of them wobbled and started to fall.

Bill saw them coming first and yelled. But instead of getting out himself, he grabbed Kyle and threw him out the door toward Macrory and Esbeth. The whole pile of oak barrels crashed down and some bounced as they hit. One shattered open, the creamy purple wine pouring out in a wave in all directions while several others tumbled across the room, just missing Win and landing on Bill, who fell beneath them as they settled.

Win's back was pressed to the barrels. He was still standing, and for the first time he looked sober and concerned, perhaps because of the amount of valuable wine being spilled. Kyle, Macrory, and Esbeth watched from the doorway. When one of the loose barrels had rolled out through the doorway, they'd had to duck out of the way.

From over the top of the toppled metal frame, Boose dragged himself upright and started to climb out from behind the rack. A gouge ran across his forehead and blood ran down in a smear that was soaking his shirt. "Just lucky, no one got hurt," he said.

Then they heard Bill's moan.

A scream from behind her spun Esbeth around. She saw Betty Sue holding her hands up to both sides of her face. "Bill," she screamed again.

"He's trapped over there under those barrels," Boose said, never the one to sugar coat anything.

From under the tumble of barrels, Esbeth could see Bill's arm lift in a feeble wave. One of the barrels seemed to lie across his chest.

"Boose, you go and call for help," Kyle said.

Boose was out the door and running over into the lab before he had to be asked twice.

"Give me a hand," Kyle said to Macrory, "but these barrels are god-awful heavy." The floor was covered in a layer of wet purple.

Betty Sue jerked into action. She spun and ran down through the fermentation room. When she got to the end, she hit the button that started the rolling door up that opened one whole end of the fermentation room.

"Honey, don't," Bill called out from under the barrels.

"Where's she going?" Macrory said. Then he turned to go help Kyle.

But Esbeth reached out and grabbed his arm. "Give this a minute," she said.

"What are you talking about? A man's hurt here."

Esbeth leaned closer. "He's just pinned under there. It's not crushing his chest or anything. Trust me. This was what I came all the way out here to tell you about."

Win started to sidle around the barrels toward the door, but Kyle called over to him. "Come on, Dad. Help me."

Win went over to stand beside his son and start rolling the first of the barrels upright.

A sound of a motor came from outside, then from the fermentation room as the fork lift rolled through at top speed with Betty Sue behind the wheel.

Macrory and Esbeth squeezed back against the wall as Betty Sue turned and the fork lift shot through the door into the barrel room. She expertly lowered the front until it was under the nearest barrel and lifted it, moved it to the side and set it down.

"She can run a fork lift," Macrory said into Esbeth's ear.

"I know. I should have known that she could in a small operation like this, and as long as she's been around. She's probably had to do a bit of everything in her day."

Esbeth was thinking back to the day of Margo's death. Betty Sue crashes their truck into a car and then in the distraction runs around through the buildings to use the fork lift to lift Margo into the auger hopper. She'd already carried the unconscious Margo that far on a two-wheeled cart, or something. The trick was getting her out to the hopper and inside with the fork lift under the cover and noise of everyone messing with the wreck. Margo gets covered up with grapes while Betty Sue is back outside with Bill and Win to straighten out the accident. As for Chaz, it would have been easy for someone like Betty Sue, a former lab technician, to get close enough to him on top of a fermentation tank to spray him with the sulphur dioxide.

The last barrel was off Bill and still resting on the fork lift when Kyle and Win rushed to help him to his feet. Once the barrels were off, he looked banged up, but okay. His shirt and jeans were soaked on the back with wine. Boose was just coming around the corner from the lab.

"Betty Sue Markley," Macrory boomed out over the noise of the fork lift's engine, "step down from there." Esbeth thought that he might just have well yelled, "You're under arrest for the murders of Margo and Chaz Castle." The response would have been the same.

Betty Sue sat at the controls and her shoulders slumped. Bill's look at her was one of horror and anguish.

Win and Kyle spun toward her at the same time. Kyle stood stunned and staring, still holding Bill upright. But Win screamed a hysterical scream and leaped at the fork lift, trying to climb over the barrel and get at Betty Sue.

She recoiled first, then hit the controls and the fork lift shot forward, smashing Win back against the other barrels and ramming the barrel he clutched against him.

Boose was across the room in a flash. He knocked Betty Sue away from the controls, and Macrory was there to grab her. Boose hit the controls and backed away slowly. The stand of barrels tottered, but didn't fall over onto Win. But he slid down the side of them, his chest visibly crushed.

Kyle rushed to him, afraid to touch him or move him.

Esbeth was there, peering in, and it was hard to tell if it was blood coming from Win's mouth, or wine. Win tried to speak, but couldn't, so he reached out a hand and clasped Kyle's arm.

Boose turned off the fork lift's engine. They could all hear Betty Sue sobbing and the sound of thick unfiltered red wine pouring slow as sludge from one of the broken barrels.

Betty Sue had quit struggling as soon as the cuffs were on, but she hung her head, cried, and would not look over at Bill. His eyes were still open wide in shock, and it was not all from having trouble breathing or speaking. He limped over closer to Betty Sue. "Why?" he said.

"You know." Her voice quivered.

"But not…"

"Let's not say anything that makes it too easy for them." She lifted her head for the first time to look at him, and all Esbeth could see on her face was the depth of love that had drove her beyond rational behavior.

Esbeth saw traces of madness too in that love, the same kind of madness that had driven Win. She wondered in a glimmer, and not for the first time, if that kind of emotional madness could be infectious. But she shook that off. Still, it was a different Betty Sue that Esbeth was seeing, different from the one she had spent so much time around. She didn't have to ask what had driven Betty Sue, and she noticed Bill didn't either. Esbeth knew that someone like Bill would let a boss with Win's forcefulness walk all over him. When Bill was demoted, his salary cut, and Chaz named winemaster, it had looked like Chaz would be even more likely to hold Bill under his foot for life. Betty Sue had cracked, had had enough of that. The greatest irony to Esbeth was that Betty Sue had been driven to the level of ruthless desperate action Win was trying to get out of his boys.

AFTER A WHILE she could hear the distant "whop, whop, whop" of the approaching StarFlight helicopter. It had only been twenty or twenty-five minutes this time. All the Castle name in the news must have speeded up the response time.

In the shuffle of loading Win onto the 'copter, the Texas Ranger eased close to Esbeth, a still somewhat unsatisfied look to the twist of his mouth.

"I guess when Bill wouldn't stand up for himself," Macrory said to Esbeth, "she was trying to make the future happen for him. The heirs didn't know squat about wine. With Chaz gone, Bill would be back in a good position, needed, valued, maybe even paid more."

Esbeth could only nod slowly.

"And Margo had to go because she was the only one pushing hard for the investigation to go the way it should, not tripping us like Win. Maybe Margo even worked through to the right conclusion ahead of us."

"That could well be," Esbeth agreed. "But if she did, it's what got her killed."

"There's one thing I want to know," Macrory said to Esbeth.

"What's that?" She turned to look up at him.

"I want to know what it was you thought you'd made a mistake about?"

"Oh, that." Esbeth waved an emotionally tired hand at him. "When you first asked me about Betty Sue as a suspect, I dismissed her because we were thinking someone had to carry Chaz to the top of the fermentation tank. When we got around that later with the atomizer, she was my top pick again, but I didn't revisit her motives for you. Then, when it looked like someone had to lift Margo over the four-foot-high steel side of the auger hopper, I had doubts again until I thought of the likelihood of her being able to operate a fork lift and it being abandoned while all of us were over looking at the wreck Betty Sue caused."

"Well, I wish you wouldn't keep these things to yourself in the future," the Ranger said.

"Oh, phooey. I've learned to keep my mind open and free, and here I'd settled on someone from the get go. That irritated me too."

"But you were right."

"Doesn't matter. It's always wrong to let your thoughts get too rigid, especially when you're my age. If I have one thing to leave you with in your job, it's that."

The sound of the 'copter landing got louder and louder until they were unable to speak.

Esbeth looked over to where Kyle leaned close to his father. He was clutching Win's hand.

As the 'copter landed and the sound of its motor lowered, Win's eyes opened wide one final time, and he quit seeing.

"I had it all wrong," Macrory said, now that he could be heard. "I wonder if he'd be alive if I hadn't been so muddled."

Esbeth shook her head, looking far more tired and old than she had in the brief time Macrory had known her. "I was the one who didn't think there would be any more killings until you finally got the handle on this mess. I'm the one who was wrong. Win Castle may not have been a very nice person. But I would never wish anyone dead."

"Oh, come on...."

Esbeth looked up at him, and her eyes welled with moisture, one tear starting down across a wrinkled cheek from the corner of her eye. "Folks think I get some sick kind of a kick out of messing around with murder. Well, I don't. I sure enough don't."

KYLE WALKED IN slow steps away from the winery. The 'copter had left, taking Bill to the hospital and his father to the morgue. Macrory's car was pulling out of the lot, heading down the lane with Betty Sue in the back seat. Still crossing the parking lot, Esbeth drug her tired feet and her rounded shadow to her car. She looked over at Kyle, wanting to say something, but she got into her car, closed the door, and started down the lane herself.

Kyle took a deep breath of the breeze that always swept up from Lake Fredonia. He stopped at the end of the rows of the vineyard, and stood looking down between the rows. From here, he could see the surface of the lake that looked blue with small whitecaps.

Gravel from running footsteps came toward him from behind, but he did not turn and look. Pearl slowed and came to stand beside him. She reached out and put an arm around him. He put his arm around her without looking at her, ashamed of the tears covering his face. But he squeezed her hip close to his.

He was the last of the adult Castles, he realized. The estate would go to Bea's kids. Then there would be new Castles running things. He hoped they would be less aggressive and competitive, though maybe it took a bit of that to survive.

All down the rows the vines were busy making grapes, seeds for the future. It was a cycle, and it wouldn't end here. He hoped it wouldn't end ever.

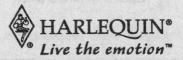

From first love to forever, these love stories
are fairy tale romances for today's woman.

Modern, passionate reads that are powerful and provocative.

Emotional, compelling stories that capture the intensity
of living, loving and creating a family in today's world.

A roller-coaster read that delivers romantic thrills
in a world of suspense, adventure and more.

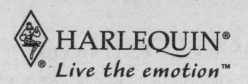
HARLEQUIN®
Live the emotion™

Upbeat,
All-American Romances

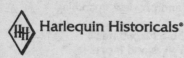
Romantic Comedy

Historical,
Romantic Adventure

Romantic Suspense

The essence of
modern romance

Seduction and passion
guaranteed

Emotional,
Exciting, Unexpected

Temptation

Sassy, Sexy, Seductive!